Discovery

Christopher Ryan

Better Than Starbucks Publications

Discovery

First Printing: ISBN 979-8-9886211-3-3

Cover image: Jake Marshall

Better Than Starbucks Publications
1524 Camino Real, Hobbs, New Mexico 88240

*For Mom,
in gratitude for all her sacrifices,
and in sorrow for all she missed
during a lifetime marked by profound change,
and for my wife Fran,
without whose creative vision and encouragement
this book would not have happened.*

ONE

Helen Bryan's dead husband Ed stood at the foot of her bed, revealed in the timid light of an early May morning. This struck her as strange. Stranger still — and more frightening — was what he said, in just above a whisper, through slightly parted lips.

"It was all a mistake."

The statement, made in Ed's familiar voice but without inflection, brought her abruptly upright. Pain lanced through her back, neck and shoulders, a reminder — as if she needed one — of the arthritis that had plagued her for the last 20 of her 85 years. She fell back on her pillow and waited for the ache to ease. When she tentatively raised her head again, Ed had gone.

She surveyed the room, her eyes darting left and right as she attempted to hold her head as still as possible, searching for the intruder in the semi-darkness. Nothing. She turned her head just enough to read the old clock radio on her bedside table: 6:14.

Her breathing slowed as the anxiety fueled by her husband's apparition and oddly threatening declaration subsided. Of course, there was no ghost delivering disturbing cryptic messages. She must have dreamed it. But the words left her shaken.

She rested her head on the pillow and lay staring at the ceiling, listening to the muted roar of Piñon Creek, the snowmelt-fed stream behind her cabin. In her mind, she watched the light of the rising sun move toward her from west to east across the San Luis Valley.

Dawn came late to her small home, where the steep western slope of the Sangre de Cristo mountains levelled as it met the valley floor. Blocked by high ridges, the rays first touched the San Juan range more than 60 miles away. A golden glow illuminated the far peaks, slipped down to flow eastward over the intervening flatland and climbed the immense jagged wall of rock. As the sun lifted over the peaks, its rays shattered in slow motion against the ridges and chasms into shards of light and shadow.

She sighed in anticipation of the hurt then rolled onto her side and let her legs fall off the edge of the bed, their weight, along with a somewhat unreliable but usually adequate push from her arms, helped pull her up to a sitting position. Grimacing, she stood, lost her balance and nearly fell, reaching out for the bedside table to steady herself. The sudden motion aggravated the pain in her hand, arm and shoulder. A small cry tried to escape her, but she suppressed it. The stiffness and discomfort would ease somewhat as the day went on. They always did.

Still using the bedside table for support, she slipped her bunioned feet into soft red slippers with pink roses on the toes. They were a gift from her eldest son Eddie, now showing loose threads at the seams and a few small holes after 10 years of wear. She lifted a bright red robe from the back of a recliner and slipped into it.

From the bed, she navigated haltingly to the maple dining table that occupied a corner of the room. It served not only as a place to eat but also as a desk and an observation post. Two large windows offered a view of her bird feeders to the north and, to the east, Piñon Creek. She lowered herself gingerly into a chair and looked out at her feeders.

The array included tubes filled with black thistle seed mixed with pale millet, several wire cages holding her homemade suet and three covered platforms offering a choice of two kinds of sunflower seeds. The first birds of the morning had arrived, so she opened her notebook and studied the list of species she'd recorded the day before. It included the usual visitors: Steller's jay, mountain chickadee, white- and red-breasted nuthatch and 10 other familiar names.

She pushed herself up from the table and turned carefully toward her small kitchen, keeping one hand on the tabletop to prevent a fall. Her balance was iffy and, as much as she hated to admit such weakness, she couldn't afford to take a tumble. She had already broken her left wrist when she toppled over in her garden almost a year ago. She knew she'd broken it, but she refused to get it set. Now, when she held out her hand palm down, it angled off rather sharply to the left. She could still use it, though, even if the arthritis made almost any motion hurt like the very devil. Fortunately, she was right-handed.

When she felt confident enough, she walked to the kitchen where she filled a tea kettle and put it on the stove to heat. She pulled a butter dish and a jar of strawberry jam from the refrigerator, placed them on the counter next to the toaster, withdrew a small plate from the cupboard and a knife and spoon from their drawer, took two slices of white bread from a plastic bag and dropped them into the toaster. The appliance worked as it had, faithfully, since 20 years before she moved to this house, automatically lowering the bread as the coils inside reddened.

It was a ritual she'd performed every morning for years, even when her sons and their families visited. They were left to make their own breakfast. She'd already done it for her boys for far too long.

The toaster clicked, rousing her from a reverie induced by the rushing creek she could see through the kitchen window, and the browned bread slices emerged. She lifted them out, inhaling the aroma, laid them on the plate and cut two pats of butter, placing one in the middle of each piece of toast to let the heat soften them. From one cupboard, she took a jar of instant decaffeinated coffee and, from another, a mug. A few minutes later, the tea kettle began whistling. She spooned coffee crystals from the jar and poured the boiling water over them, stirring until they dissolved.

The coffee would be too hot to drink just yet, so she spread the butter on her toast and smeared each slice with jam. Her meal prepared, she carried the plate and mug to the table and sat, pausing to study the feeders before she ate.

The light had grown stronger, and more birds had arrived. They included the regulars: a Steller's jay quarrelling with a black-billed magpie over the best perch on a platform full of sunflower seeds, a white-breasted nuthatch on a suet cage and dark-eyed juncos on the ground pecking at seeds dropped from the feeders overhead. Nothing new, but she dutifully recorded each species in her notebook before taking her first bite of toast and sip of coffee.

Although she was close enough to the birds to make binoculars unnecessary, she picked up the pair of Bausch & Lombs she'd had since her husband had given them to her more than 50 years earlier and focused on the Steller's jay and the magpie. Their combat over the seeds offered an opportunity to appreciate their beauty as well as their pugnacious nature. Because they were both common in this part of Colorado, it was easy to take them for granted, as people who live by the ocean can grow accustomed to it and lose sight of its grandeur.

She noted the Steller's jay's dark head with its substantial crest and how the color transitioned to blue as it moved down the bird's body. Its forehead sported two vertical white stripes that gave it a clownish look, accentuated by white eyelids and a touch of white under the eyes.

For its part, the larger, heavier magpie flashed broad white wing patches and a white belly that contrasted sharply with its black head, neck and breast. It's blue wings and long blue tail might have rendered it almost regal if it weren't for its thuggish behavior.

After a minute or so, she shifted the binoculars to the suet feeder, which the white-breasted nuthatch now shared with its red-breasted cousin. The white-breasted nuthatch was among her favorites, mostly because of its call, a quiet kind of chuckle she often heard while working in the garden or walking in the woods that surrounded the house. All year, she could count on the nuthatches to bring a little cheer into her life, at least until her hearing started to go.

She put the binoculars down and took another bite of toast and sip of coffee. The coffee would be cold soon, so she took three large swallows followed by another bite of toast.

She still had the toast in her mouth when movement in the lower limbs of a still-leafless river birch beyond the bank of feeders caught her eye. An unfamiliar small bird flew from the birch to one of the thistle-seed feeders, landed on a perch, quickly surveyed the area for threats and began pecking out a meal.

She put her toast down, picked up the binoculars and locked in on the stranger.

"It was all a mistake."

Her husband's voice spoke the words, not loudly but distinctly, and she turned — too quickly — to find him, forgetting for a moment that he'd been dead more than 20 years. All she saw, as she grimaced at the pain in her neck and back, was her husband's portrait hanging over the bed she'd shared with him in another place and time and where she now slept alone.

The photograph showed a man in his 50s, black hair tinged with gray — cut short but still full — sitting at a desk, holding a pipe in his right hand. His smile revealed even, white teeth and added charm to a handsome Irish face with a few wrinkles in all the right places around the eyes and mouth. It was a face you could trust, perfect for a physician.

Feeling foolish even as she did it, she asked the portrait, "What was a mistake?" Then she shook her head, feeling the pain but almost grateful for its reality, and returned her attention to the new bird, lifting the binoculars to her eyes. Something tickled her right cheek, and she pulled the binoculars away, using her finger to brush off whatever it was. The finger came away wet. She looked down at her hand to see what it was, and a drop of liquid hit the table, shattering into a many-pointed star. It was followed by another and another, and she realized she was crying.

"Hell's bells." She put the binoculars down as a fist closed around her diaphragm and squeezed a gasping sob from deep in her chest. Elbows on the table, hands over her eyes pressing hard to stem the flow of tears, she wept.

TWO

She knew she'd been crying but had no idea why — except it must have had something to do with the mysterious "mistake." A quick glance at the clock radio told her she'd been weeping for at least 15 minutes, and that embarrassed her. She'd never been one to indulge in self-pity, and this felt like she'd immersed herself in it and gone for a long swim. It was silly, really. She had a good life. No worries about money, a home in her favorite place on earth, children who were far from perfect but who seemed to care about her. Comparatively speaking, she was lucky.

She plucked a paper napkin from a holder and wiped her face and the tabletop clear of tears. Through the window, she saw that the new bird was still at the feeder. So she put the binoculars to her eyes and studied it.

For a moment, she wished she had Ed's camera and heavy 500mm lens he'd carried everywhere because photographing birds without it was next to impossible. She remembered how intrepid he'd looked with the camera and its huge lens on a tripod he'd rest on his shoulder as he walked. But she hadn't learned anything about photography and had never owned a camera. Ed's was now with one of the boys. She didn't know which.

But she did know that the bird she was looking at was a Passerine — a songbird. A wave of avian anatomical terms surged from memory, and she lowered the binoculars so she could take notes. She pulled the notebook closer and picked up the pen. Quickly, she jotted a list:

Size: tree sparrow
Lateral crown stripes: black
Median crown stripe: yellow
Superciliums: white
Supralorals: white
Lores: yellow
Upper mandible: black
Lower mandible: black
Throat: white
Malars: white
Auriculars: white

Lateral throat stripes: black
Nape: brown
Eyelines: brown
Breast: white
Sides, flanks, belly: white
Scapulars: black
Mantle: white
Median coverts: white
Greater coverts, primary coverts, tertials, secondaries,
Primaries: brown
Tail: reddish brown
Undertail coverts: white

It wasn't complete. She could have gone into much more detail. But it was enough to jog her memory, should it be necessary. The yellow median crown stripe and lores ought to be enough to cinch an identification, but it couldn't hurt to have more.

It had been a long time since she'd used the more technical terms to describe a bird's anatomy, and she was surprised at how quickly they came to mind. She had her ornithology professor to thank for it, although she harbored bad memories of him. He'd told her she was the best student he'd had. At age 55, after leaving the state university to marry Ed 35 years earlier, she'd basked in his praise. She couldn't foresee the attack to come.

She picked up her tattered copy of Roger Tory Peterson's *A Field Guide to Western Birds* that she and Ed had used for at least 40 years and began leafing through the pages of illustrations, trying to identify the new bird. She had never seen this species before, but from its appearance and behavior she knew it would likely fall into one of two genera: *Carpodacus* — finches, or *Aimophila* — sparrows. She would focus on those two categories first. She turned to the finches.

"It was all a mistake."

The voice wasn't Ed's this time. It belonged to Robert Beekman, her ornithology professor, someone she did not want echoing in her head. The last time he'd spoken to her, he'd left her feeling he'd stolen every joy and purpose she'd ever experienced. Remembering, she clenched her fists and slammed them down on the field guide. She swiped at the tears that welled up and spilled down her cheeks, catching them before they could fall to the table, and used a napkin to wipe her face and hands, as if to scrub away a stain.

Once more with the binoculars to her eyes, she stared at the bird without seeing it, picturing instead the small wetland near her home where she'd chosen to do her fieldwork. She loved the place and spent as much time as she could there while her project lasted.

Rich with the odors of decay and rebirth, the wetland, with its cattails, sedges, marsh milkweed, smartweed, and arrowhead as cover, provided a home for creatures of all kinds, from microbes, worms and insects to mammals, reptiles, amphibians, fish and, of course, birds. Life swarmed there, yet despite the mortal struggles she knew took place night and day within the vegetation, a quietness prevailed, a peace that belied the mayhem.

She'd studied the wetland for a year, from late spring to late spring, watching and recording the comings and goings of birds that passed through on migration as well as the species that came to nest, raise a brood or two and then migrate, and those that remained year-round. She'd noted their feeding habits, mating rituals, how they went about building nests and raising young and anything else that defined them as members of a particular species.

She heard the call that second spring — a series of *keks*, the volume diminishing as the call reached its close. It arose from a hidden place among the reeds, and she knew from listening for hours to birdcall recordings that it could belong to only two species: king or clapper rail. Either bird would be an important find in eastern Kansas, where she and Ed had settled and raised their family.

A quick look at her Peterson guide told her the chances of the bird being a clapper rail were remote, at best. The clapper's range included almost exclusively coastal areas. Its preferred habitat was salt marshes.

The king rail, on the other hand, had been seen, though rarely, through-out the eastern half of the U.S. It liked fresh as well as brackish swamps and marshes. All the evidence pointed its way. Excited at her find, she hurried home to call Professor Beekman.

His reaction disappointed her. "Did you actually see it? Are you sure it wasn't a frog or something?"

"I only heard it. But that call is pretty distinctive."

During the pause that followed, she could hear his breathing. "I need to check this out. I'll meet you there."

She arrived at the wetland before Beekman and returned to the spot where she first heard the rail. The *kek* call sounded from the reeds, and she used her binoculars to scan the area where she thought it originated. No rail, but the call came again just as Beekman pulled up to park beside her car. He approached her slowly, as if concerned that he might disturb the bird. The rail had fallen silent. The professor stood beside her, his binoculars at the ready.

"It called just as you drove up," she whispered.

"All right," he said in a normal tone of voice. "Let's see what we have here."

He took a few steps closer to the edge of the marsh. Tentatively, she followed, not sure if the movement would disturb the rail, wanting it to call one more time before it scurried away to hide elsewhere within the jungle of water-loving plants. It would be far more likely to attempt an escape that way than to fly.

Beekman stared out at the marsh. "Where did you say you heard it?"

She stopped next to him and pointed. "Out there about twenty yards."

He trained his binoculars on the area she indicated and began scanning it. "Nope. Nothing."

"I'm sure it'll call again."

"Maybe." He lowered his binoculars and let them hang from the strap around his neck. "I'll give it a few more minutes. Then I have to get back for a department meeting."

For someone who had to hear the bird for himself, he seemed to be in a hurry to leave.

"I know what I heard, Professor Beekman."

He swung toward her, a tight smile failing to soften the look of tried patience he'd worn since his arrival. "A king rail would be quite unusual here. You have to have confirmation — in this case, my confirmation."

He turned back to face the marsh. She bit her lip, angry and embarrassed by the unexpected rebuke from a man who, up until this moment, had offered nothing but praise for her work.

Beekman raised his binoculars and scanned the marsh again. "I guess your rail has decided not to let anyone but you know it's around."

"Are you saying I'm making it up?"

"I really don't know. What I do know is you can't count a king rail until you have my confirmation. And right now, I don't have time to stand around waiting." He turned and started to walk toward his car.

"Stop."

He did, as if he'd hit a wall, and turned around, his face red, his smile, such as it had been, gone. "You don't speak to me that way. Now go back to your nice house and your husband the doctor. I'm tired of watching you treat ornithology like a pastime. If you want to be a birdwatcher, fine, just don't waste my time with your little hobby."

He left her staring after him as he returned to his car and drove away, leaving a trail of dust. As the cloud settled to the ground, the rail called.

THREE

She didn't know how long she'd been gazing through her binoculars at an empty finch feeder, but the new bird had disappeared. She lowered the binoculars and tried to locate it at another feeder then raised them again and examined the river birch where it had first emerged. It was gone, maybe for good.

The thought that the bird might have disappeared forever nearly brought her to tears again, but she fought them back. She had enough information to identify the silly thing, so if she couldn't find it in her field guide, she'd try other sources. After all, it was spring. This could be a molting bird in transition from non-breeding to breeding plumage. Or it might be a first-year juvenile. Her Peterson guide offered no help with juveniles or differences between breeding and non-breeding birds. It was time for a visit to the Valley View Public Library.

She must have been sitting still longer than she realized because getting out of her chair was more difficult and painful than she thought it would be. When she stood, finally, she held on to the edge of the table and the back of her chair until the wobblies subsided. Taking small steps to retain her balance, she walked to the kitchen, lifted her car keys from a hook on the wall and left through the door that opened to the deck overlooking the creek. Using every handhold she could find, she made her way to the garage where her 27-year-old Chevy Blazer sat waiting.

Over the past few years, as her mobility had become more limited, she'd figured out a technique for getting into the old Blazer. She grasped the steering wheel, lifted her right leg to place her right foot on the running board and pulled herself onto the seat. Then she dragged first her right leg then her left under the steering wheel. The maneuver seemed to get more difficult every time she used the car, buts it still worked, and she figured it would for a while longer. But, lord, it hurt.

A few deep, pain-abating breaths later, she backed out of the garage and onto the quarter-mile road that would take her to the town's main thoroughfare, a two-lane blacktop on which traffic of any kind came as a surprise.

She drove through Valley View's town center, which consisted of a small hardware store and lumber yard, a six-room inn with an attached liquor store named Twenty-first Amendment, an empty former video rental shop, a grocery store/gas station called Valley View Market, the shabby offices of the monthly *Valley View Mountaineer,* staffed solely by its editor and publisher Janet Lambert, and the Double Dyke Bakery and Coffee House.

The latter establishment's owners — Minnie McFadden and Tilly Renquist, gray-haired and obviously fans of their own baking — had been partners for 30 years and a married couple since such an alliance became legal. Helen didn't understand lesbians, but she did appreciate the Double Dyke's croissants, especially with some butter and strawberry jam. The women's sex life was their business, though she wished they'd keep it to themselves instead of advertising it in big letters on the front of their shop. But the croissants were another thing entirely, creating a space untouched by her moral judgment and open to moments of delight.

However, she was on a mission to identify the new bird. So she left the bakery behind and passed Sheriff Ethan MacGregor in his patrol car beginning his twice-monthly Valley View checkup.

The sheriff's jurisdiction included Saguache County, covering the northern half of the San Luis Valley. Although the county encompassed more than 3,000 square miles, its population was only 6,000. Sheriff MacGregor had a lot of ground to cover but not many citizens to keep safe. His primary task in Valley View was making sure the residents, mostly retirees, were still breathing and hadn't yet lost their marbles.

She watched in her rearview mirror as the sheriff stopped in front of the newspaper office and unfolded his tall, rather thin frame from the driver's seat. With his dark hair and square-jawed face, he looked a bit like Ed, but he was considerably taller. Janet told her once that he always checked in with her for information about any odd behavior before continuing his patrol.

She rounded the first of two sharp bends that took her out into the valley as the sheriff entered the newspaper office. After the second bend, she crossed Piñon Creek making its way onto the valley floor where it grew narrower and shallower until, a couple of miles out, it disappeared into the sandy soil. All the streams flowing out of the Sangre de Cristos faced the same fate, a wild, snowmelt-fed beginning from a lake high among the peaks to a trickling end marked by the disappearance of a shrinking line of cottonwood trees.

Shortly after leaving the bridge over Piñon Creek, she was in the valley proper. Except where the various streams flowed, there were few trees. In this part of the country, trees occupied a narrow band between the valley and timberline. Where the forest met the valley, it looked as if an ocean of rabbit brush had run up against a sinuous beachline.

Three miles beyond the pines and cottonwoods that marked the forest's last stand, she parked in front of the Valley View Public Library. The building was once a clubhouse for golfers and tennis players taking advantage of the nine-hole course and the courts belonging to the Baca Grande Resort. The resort lasted a few years before it starved to death for lack of guests — a demise that surprised no one except, apparently, the owners.

She remembered when the place seemed to be a going concern. The restaurant was decent then. She and Ed and her youngest boys ate there a few times. The food was unremarkable, but the hundreds of violet-green swallows that made their home under the hotel's eaves provided plenty of entertainment as they swooped and dove to catch flying insects. She could have watched them for hours and now wondered where they'd gone since the main building, with its guest rooms and restaurant, shut down.

When she'd first moved to Valley View after Ed died, she'd been able to play tennis for the first time in several years, thanks to a hip replacement. The stroke that killed her husband took the better part of a year to do the job. During that time, she'd cared for him on her own, lifting him, helping him walk as he leaned on her. Before long, the pain in her left hip became almost unbearable, and X-rays showed why. Arthritis and stress had nearly destroyed the joint.

The surgery went well, and recovery took less time than she feared it would. A year after Ed's death, she left her home of 40-plus years and settled in Valley View where her husband, free of the demands of his work, had seemed most relaxed and happy. She'd hoped the two of them could share the house and make it their home, and she'd ordered renovations shortly after Ed's stroke with that goal in mind.

Although they'd avoided discussing it as they grew older, she knew Ed didn't want to retire. She suspected his reluctance stemmed more from pride than love of being a physician. He had stature in their small town and didn't want to give it up. The way he saw it, retirement meant relinquishing his identity.

But the stroke changed all that. She knew everyone in the family except Ed could see him losing touch for at least a year leading up to it. But no one said anything. When she thought about that time, she felt sick with shame and guilt. If only she'd had the courage to confront the signs head-on, maybe things would have been different.

Something was obviously wrong. One night, at dinner, when three of the boys and their wives were visiting, Ed regaled the table with news of his own latest physical exam. But he focused on his eyesight, bragging about his 20/20 vision, repeating himself at least five times. It was as if the entire exam boiled down to one thing — how well he could see. Nothing else mattered. She and the rest of the family stared at their plates and pushed their food around as Ed rambled on.

When Ed stopped talking, they cleared the table and said not a word about the demented soliloquy they'd just experienced. Later, as her husband snored beside her, she wept.

Things grew worse as the year wore on. Ed started drinking more, and the alcohol only added to his memory lapses and confusion. She worried about the effect his condition might have on his patients and the consequences if he made a serious medical error.

At the same time, she couldn't talk to him or anyone else about the problem. Instead, she'd make excuses for him — he was just tired; he had too much to do and was having trouble keeping it all straight. She would wait to see if it got worse before saying anything that might upset him.

Then, on a warm day in April, Ed decided to trim some dead branches from one of the weeping willows in their backyard. He climbed onto a lower limb and began sawing a branch. She could see him from the kitchen window and hoped he didn't fall. Rather than worry about it, she found something else to do and put the situation out of sight and mind.

A half-hour later, she heard an odd scuffling and grunting, like an animal searching for food in the plastic bags of garbage they kept in the garage until trash day to avoid just that kind of problem. Deciding Ed had left the door open and a dog had taken advantage of the opportunity, she grabbed a broom and hurried downstairs to chase it away.

When she pulled open the door to the garage, she found Ed on the concrete floor, his right arm and leg churning, his left arm and leg unnaturally limp and still. He was looking at her, his eyes frantic. The left side of his face seemed to have melted, his mouth sagging and his left eyelid drooping so his eye was almost hidden as if by a horrifying extended wink.

She knelt at his side as his right leg and arm continued to churn uselessly, and his awful grunting rose in volume. Then the grunts became slurred words. She bent closer to try to understand what he was saying.

"Help me." The request seemed to take all the will he had, and he fell back. She couldn't raise him from the floor to his feet, so, even though she knew it would make him angry, she decided to take charge of the situation.

"I'm calling an ambulance."

The eye that still opened widened, and the fear that was already present grew more obvious.

"No, wait. Just a minute." His voice was weaker now, and the slurred words were more difficult to decipher.

"No, Ed, I can't. You're in trouble."

Surely he knew what was happening to him and that he had to get help. He was a doctor, for God's sake.

"I'll be back in a second. I have to get to the phone." She touched his face and got up quickly, almost running to the door, but trying not to show how close to panic she felt.

When she returned, he was lying quiet, his face still malformed on the left side. At first, she thought he might be dead, and she knelt beside him, bending down to check his heartbeat and breathing. He was alive, though his breaths were rapid and seemed shallow.

She followed the ambulance to the hospital in her car rather than riding with Ed because she didn't want to be without transportation. Her ability to make decisions surprised her. She felt remarkably clear-headed, given the circumstances. She focused on the ambulance making its way the short distance to the hospital, as if it were a beacon guiding her.

At the hospital, she parked as close as she could to the emergency entrance where the ambulance pulled up to unload its passenger. She watched as the crew pushed the gurney through the doors, attended by a nurse and a doctor. Ed was connected to an IV, and he lay terribly still.

She sat for a while, using her car as a refuge while she tried to understand what had just happened. It might have been a relief to cry, but she couldn't. The tears wouldn't come, only ragged intakes of breath that might have been sobs but sounded more like the grunting noises Ed had been making when she found him. After a few minutes, she climbed out of the car and entered the hospital.

From her seat in the waiting area, she could see the ER doctor working on Ed, who was hooked up to monitors and still attached to the IV. She thought it must be a hard thing to treat a fellow physician whose illness was obviously serious, possibly fatal.

The realization that Ed might die hit her hard. Until now, she'd been dealing with his problem from moment to moment, all her attention concentrated on getting him the help he needed. She hadn't considered that all she did could come to nothing in the end.

Of course, Ed would be all right. He would come back from this and be better than he was before it happened. It was only fair, after all. He deserved a life with her, living through their later years watching birds and being together. He was only 67 years old, damn it. Just 67 years old. Death was a long way off yet.

At long last, two attendants wheeled Ed out of the treatment bay and into an elevator. The doctor who had been caring for him approached her and introduced himself.

"Your husband has suffered a cerebral hemorrhage. The bleeding has resulted in paralysis on his left side, so the hemorrhage is on the right. Surgery might be necessary to stop the bleeding. Right now, it looks as though the bleeding has slowed or even stopped."

She felt a tremor of hope. Maybe this wasn't as bad as it looked.

When he saw her brighten, he shifted gears. "But even if the hemorrhaging has stopped, it has caused damage to his brain."

"Okay. What does that mean?"

"It means an extended and difficult recovery. And even then, the long-term effects could be life-altering — persistent weakness, if not paralysis, cognitive problems and other issues. He'll need a lot of care, perhaps for the rest of his life."

"Well, aren't you a ray of sunshine."

He gave her a smile tinged with chagrin.

"I'm sorry. I know this is a lot to take in, but I don't want to give you the wrong idea. Your husband is very ill. We'll do everything we can for him, but I want to make sure you understand the situation."

He took her hand in both of his. "You don't know me, but I've worked with your husband for ten years. I'm a big fan, and I'm sorry this happened."

"I understand. Thank you."

She hurried away, feeling the need to escape this threat to Ed's future — and hers. In the elevator, she reached toward the panel of buttons and realized she didn't know which floor to choose. She caught the doors before they could close and walked back to the ER where she found the doctor who had first seen Ed. She'd forgotten his name, so she sneaked a peek at his nametag before asking him where she could find her husband.

"Intensive care. Third floor."

After all the years she'd been with Ed, she realized in that moment that she had never known what he did. It was a strange awakening, as if she'd just opened her eyes to confront a dark chasm of ignorance. She'd never talked to him about his work beyond asking how his day had been. And he never responded beyond "Hectic." or "Long." or "Okay." Of whatever medical triumphs or defeats he'd faced, she knew nothing. He was often gone from early morning until late evening, running his private practice. Huge parts of his life were a mystery to her.

She wondered how much of his life Ed had spent seeing patients in the ICU, how he behaved with them, how they responded to him, if they could. What did he do when one of them died? Did he close their eyes? What was the ritual?

In her time, she'd lost a brother, both parents, both Ed's parents and other friends and relatives. She had been an observer, though, never a participant. She'd stayed in the background, often not being present at the moment of death because she had to take care of the children.

What would she do if Ed died? She would have to be by his side. That's what wives and husbands did for each other. The thought felt like a heavy shroud descending, smothering her.

By the time the elevator doors opened to the ICU, she was ready to turn around and go home. It would be the responsible thing to do, after all. She had people to call, not only her sons but also a large number of relatives and friends who needed to know what had happened. It would take hours to get through the list. But she approached the nurse's station and asked for the room number. Alone, she walked down the hall, dreading what she was about to see.

Ed lay on his back, his eyes closed, an oxygen mask covering his nose and mouth, monitors displaying his heartbeat and other vital information. He looked peaceful, more relaxed than she'd seen him in a long while. She wasn't sure what she'd been expecting. It wasn't as if he'd been in an awful auto accident, bruised, cut and broken. He'd managed to get down from the tree without injuring himself and made it a couple of hundred feet to the garage.

But he looked so small.

She drew up a chair and sat beside the bed, studying his face, willing him to open his eyes and tell her everything would be all right. When no miracle occurred, she took his right hand and squeezed it. No response. She let his hand drop to the bed and sat back.

Since she'd found him in the garage, she hadn't shed a tear, and none came now. She leaned back and stared at the ceiling, exhaustion leaving her limp.

"If you're going to die, please do it soon."

For a second, she thought she'd said the words out loud, and her hands flew to cover her mouth. She glanced at Ed, who remained unmoving except for the rise and fall of his breathing.

She couldn't escape the desire to be anywhere but in that room. In her mind she had betrayed her husband, the man she'd loved for so many years. Still, she couldn't deny the urge to run away.

She left the room, stopping again at the nurse's station to explain that she had to contact a lot of people. She would be back later and asked that someone call her right away if anything changed.

The setting sun enriched the purple of the blossoms on the redbud trees and highlighted the pale green of new leaves opening on the sycamores and oaks around the hospital parking lot. She heard cardinals and robins singing and grackles squawking as they searched the grass for seeds and bugs.

After getting into the car and closing the door, she screamed, giving voice to her grief and a rage she could no longer contain.

Drained, she started the car and drove home. The tears would not come. They wouldn't for a long time.

FOUR

At the Valley View Public Library, Helen struggled a little to get out of the Blazer, but she succeeded at last and walked stiffly to the library door, carrying her notebook. She entered to find Matt Enfield at a table, reading a large volume. He looked up when she walked in.

"Well, if isn't the bird lady."

"How are you, Matt?"

"Getting by. Yourself?"

"The same."

Their conversations seldom varied much from this formula. The niceties completed, she walked past him into the rather barren stacks to find what she was looking for — a bird guide that was less than 50 years old.

According to Janet, who had come to know him suspiciously well, Matt Enfield had arrived in Saguache County about two years before, just out of the army after serving in Afghanistan. He came with only his uniform to wear and a little cash from his last paycheck. For a while, he lived in his car until he managed to land a job managing the county landfill.

With the money he earned, he expanded his wardrobe to include two pairs of blue jeans, new underwear and socks, two western-style shirts, work gloves, winter gloves, a light jacket and a heavy coat. For shoes, he made do with his service footwear. It was Janet's intimate knowledge of Matt's wardrobe that led Helen to suspect they were more than casual acquaintances.

She first saw Matt before he'd started work at the landfill, so the initial impression wasn't good. He was clean enough but always wore the same clothes, and they were a bit worn. She had to admit he looked much better in new jeans and a new shirt. She and Matt had settled into a cordial, if not quite warm, relationship that had not yet varied from the script.

Meeting new people was always difficult for Helen. It took a while for her to trust someone enough to move beyond pleasantries into more substantial interaction. She preferred to keep her life confidential, allowing her acquainttances to skim the surface, like a stone skipping across a pond, but always disengaging before it had a chance to sink. Years of being a doctor's wife, forced to be present when called upon for events, had taught her how to negotiate traps that might cause her to reveal more than she wished to share while remaining gracious. It was hard work, but it was her duty.

Among the people she knew in Valley View, she had allowed only Janet to plumb the depths and only so far. She supposed she could count the owner of the *Valley View Mountaineer* a friend. So far, the pretty, dark-haired woman had kept her distance, despite being a reporter and therefore a natural snoop.

Janet knew about Ed and the boys and their wives and kids as well as Helen's interest in birds. It was all she needed to know, at least for the foreseeable future. The temptation to say too much and allow emotions to get in the way sometimes arose, but she held it down, wrestling the demon into submission with an ease born of long practice.

Janet, on the other hand, wore her heart not only on her sleeve but all over her, as though she'd been slimed, like the kids Helen had seen when she accidentally tuned in to the nauseating spectacle on a children's television show. Janet loved to share the slime, some of it, in Helen's opinion, better kept to herself. But the rules of graciousness demanded listening and nodding, no matter how strong the need to escape.

Still, she liked Janet, in spite of her penchant for saying too much, and she enjoyed their infrequent visits, especially during the winter when the short days and long, cold nights isolated her. During those months, she'd watch TV, feed the birds and worry that she'd lose the ability to talk. Only a few calls from her sons and Janet's over-sharing, as Helen's kids called it, kept her able to form words.

From a shelf, she pulled two volumes: *The Sibley Field Guide to Birds of Western North America* and *The Sibley Guide to Bird Life & Behavior.* It was a good place to start. She sat at a table some distance from Matt and opened the western bird guide to "Finches and Old World Sparrows."

The illustrations and descriptions in the Sibley guide offered a good deal more information than she could get from Peterson. She studied the pictures of adult males and females as well as juveniles and first-winter birds, along with variations in plumage that could make identification challenging.

None of the finch species matched her memory or her notes, so she moved on to "Emberizine Sparrows and Their Allies," which included, in addition to sparrows, the towhees, buntings, juncos and longspurs. Same story. A look at tanagers and flycatchers offered nothing more promising.

She knew there were ways to use a computer to help identify birds but, despite her sons' encouragement, she'd never tried one. Books were the tools she'd preferred all her life, and learning a new way of doing something she already felt comfortable doing her way seemed like a waste of time and a potential source of frustration.

More excited than disappointed by her failure to identify the new bird, she closed the guides and stood, pushing the chair with the back of her knees while keeping her hands on the table to steady herself. When she felt sure of her balance, she walked toward the door, past Matt, who still pored over his book, his profile inviting comparison with some of the Native Americans she'd seen on a trip to Arizona with Ed years ago. She decided not to disturb him and left the library.

The bright sunlight fell from a sky that still surprised her with its deep azure hue, so unlike the pale dome in the more humid region where she'd lived most of her life. Once back in her car, she sat for a moment, deciding what to do next. She needed help she couldn't find in the books she had available, so she'd have to rely on someone with skills she didn't have. skillsShe'd be foolish not to take advantage of a computer's power, so, as much as she hated the idea of letting anyone else know about the new bird, she settled on Janet. She was the only person in Valley View she thought she could risk trusting — trust that could only be meted out sparingly.

She drove back into town and parked in front of the newspaper office. When she entered, carrying her notebook, Janet was working at her computer. Without looking to see who had entered, she held up a finger.

"Just a second."

Helen remained silent as Janet's fingers flew over the keyboard, and she envied the younger woman's speed and dexterity. Her own arthritic hands would not work nearly as well.

Soon, Janet ended her typing with a slight flourish and turned in her chair.

"Hi, there."

"Hi. I'm here to ask a favor."

"Okay. How are you?"

"Fine. I need you to help me find something on the computer, if you have time."

Janet gave her a warm smile that made her already attractive face even prettier. "Glad to. Come on over here and have a seat."

She pulled another chair nearer her own and swiveled her seat a quarter turn so she was again facing the computer.

Making her way around the counter that separated Janet's work area from the rest of the room, Helen navigated past stacks of *Valley View Mountaineer* issues to take her place next to Janet, who gazed at her, apparently waiting for direction.

"I'm looking for a bird."

Janet laughed, lighting up her green eyes. "You're always looking for a bird."

"But this one is different."

"Different how?"

"I've never seen one like it before."

"Oh, wow. I'd have thought you'd seen just about every bird around here."

"Not this one."

"Okay, let's get started with a Google search."

"What?'

"A computer search. We're sure to find something on the Web."

"The what?"

Janet moved some kind of device next to her keyboard and punched it with her index finger. It clicked, and the word "Google" popped up on the computer screen above an elongated box. A vertical line blinked at the box's left end.

She looked at Janet, wanting to know how to proceed. Janet seemed surprised.

"Oh, sweetie, you've never used one of these at all, have you?"

"No. I don't like computers."

"How would you know if you've never used one?"

"I like books."

"So do I, but as aggravating as these things are — and they can be maddening — they do help." She smiled, a bit condescendingly, Helen thought, then said, "Okay. What can you tell me about this bird?"

Checking her notes, Helen selected the two field marks she thought were most likely to identify the new bird.

"It has a yellow median crown stripe and yellow lores."

"What's the second thing?"

"Lores." She spelled the word. Janet typed "birds in Colorado with yellow median crown stripe and yellow lores" into the box on the screen and tapped a key. "Images of birds in Colorado with yellow median crown stripe and yellow lores" popped into view. Below the words were photos of four birds, none of which had both a yellow median crown stripe and yellow lores.

Something else caught Helen's eye and she drew a sharp breath. "Two million twenty thousand results?"

Janet laughed. "Don't worry, none of them matter beyond the first page or so." She reached for the gizmo beside the keyboard, pressed it and moved it slightly to the left. A little arrow appeared on the screen and floated over to the line of type starting with "Images." Janet pressed on the left side of the gizmo, and the screen filled immediately with photos of birds, some of which had either yellow lores or a yellow median crown stripe but not both. Most of them had neither.

Janet turned to her. "See anything?"

"Nothing like the bird at my feeder."

"Okay, let's move on."

For the next 15 minutes, she studied screen after screen filled with images of birds. The closest she could come to the new one outside her window that morning were the white-crowned sparrow and the savannah sparrow.

She would have identified both of them immediately. Besides, neither had a yellow median crown stripe. Beyond that, the white-crowned sparrow's supralorals were yellow, not its lores. The golden-crowned sparrow showed gold only on its forecrown, and the golden-crowned kinglet was too small and also didn't have yellow lores. And, again, she would have known those birds by sight. She'd seen them many times before.

She shook her head. "This is getting me nowhere."

"Are there other markings that might be more helpful?"

"No." She stood and walked around the counter toward the door. Then she stopped and turned to Janet. "Thanks for doing this."

Janet's smile was as warm as before. "Any time. You just say the word."

"Please don't tell anyone about the bird."

The smile disappeared for a moment. "I won't. But are you okay?"

"Sure. Why?"

The smile returned, but it seemed a little forced. "Oh, nothing. We should get together at the Double Dyke for a coffee and croissant."

"Maybe next week."

"I'll call you."

"Do that." Helen waved over her shoulder as she walked out the door.

Back in the Blazer, she decided to stop to check her P.O. box, so she drove the few hundred feet to the post office. Inside, confronted by a wall filled with rows of boxes, she realized she didn't know which one was hers. She stood still and let her eyes rove over the identical brass doors, continuing to draw a blank.

Frantically, she searched her memory for a number or a location that would take her to her mail. Nothing. The woman at the counter might be able to help her, but she wasn't about to ask. This was just too embarrassing. She decided to leave and come back later. As she pushed the glass door to exit the building, a number popped into her head: 236.

That was it. With renewed confidence, she retraced her steps, pulling a key from her jacket pocket, and walked directly to Box 236. She hesitated just a second before inserting the key, then pushed it into the lock and turned it. It worked. She pulled the door open and took out her mail — a few catalogues, an electric bill and an *Audubon* magazine. Except for the magazine, her favorite because of the beautiful photographs of birds and other animals, it was hardly worth the effort, not to mention the consternation.

Energized by her victory over the mailbox number memory lapse, she drove next to the Valley View Market. She needed more strawberry jam, and there was no reason to make another trip for it.

At the store, she wondered, as she often did, how it stayed open. The owners, Joe and Pippa Jackson, kept the place stocked, but just barely. The meat was frozen, the fresh fruits and vegetables long past earning the adjective, and the rest of the merchandise kept to a minimum — a few canned goods, a sparse selection of candy and gum, some cleaning supplies. But they always had enough strawberry jam and white bread. She bought both and headed home.

Outside, she walked past the gas pumps, noting the exorbitant prices. The nearest alternative source of gasoline required a 12-mile drive to the main highway. Most of the retirees would rather get their fuel closer to home, so they paid. She was pretty sure gasoline was the Jacksons' principal source of income.

She pulled herself up into the Blazer and started to back out of her parking space. She stepped hard on the brake when tires screeched behind her. But she was too late. The collision, though hardly violent, rocked her and caused pain in her arthritic joints, especially her neck and shoulders. She rested her head on the steering wheel, partly to recover, partly out of chagrin.

Then Janet was at the window, knocking and asking if she was all right. She sat up straight and rolled down the window.

"I'm fine. Did I hit you?"

"Yeah, but I don't think it's a big deal. Hardly a scratch on either of us."

"It was my fault. I just pulled out without looking."

"I do it all the time. Who expects traffic in Valley View?"

"I should be more careful. I'll get my insurance information for you." She reached for the glove box. Janet touched her arm.

"How about we just let it go? No harm done. No reason to risk getting your rates raised. These insurance companies are the devil's spawn, right?"

"Are you sure?"

"I'm sure. Let me move my car so you can get out of here."

While she waited, Helen left the window down and listened to the wind whispering through the pines around the store, a sound that had grown fainter and fainter because of her diminishing hearing. The cottonwoods hadn't yet leafed out. When they did, in a few weeks, the wind would cause the leaves to rattle like rain on a roof during a gusty thunderstorm. These sounds always soothed her when she felt upset.

It was a good thing she'd hit Janet instead of someone else. Otherwise, she'd have to confess her guilt to a stranger and answer a lot of questions. She knew what everyone would think. She shouldn't be driving. She's too old. Her reaction time is too slow. She forgets to look for other cars. Someone should take her keys.

They would be wrong, of course. Everybody gets distracted once in a while. She would just have to pay more attention.

She made sure to check her rearview mirrors before slowly backing out of her parking place. Janet had pulled forward and stopped, so Helen gave her a little wave as she drove away.

It would be good to get home where she didn't have to deal with other people. She found even interactions not involving fender-benders exhaust-

ting. Not that she couldn't carry them off. She could, and quite effectively, but found coming up with the right words at the right time hard work. She had no idea how people could talk to each other for hours and still smile and laugh.

Her own conversations, when she didn't feel pressured to perform, tended to be filled with long pauses as she tried to formulate the right sequence of words and phrases. With strangers, especially, she fell back on a script like the one she used with Matt. If the interaction threatened to go on too long, she'd ask questions, putting the burden of continuing onto the person she was talking to. She'd found that, unlike her, other people liked to talk about themselves. She could just nod and smile and let them prattle on. In the time before Ed's death, she'd survived many a cocktail party using this tactic.

When she turned onto her private road, she was feeling better. She pulled into the garage, maneuvered her way out of the Blazer and retrieved her groceries and notebook from the backseat. As she walked past the feeders and onto her back deck, she hummed a tune. Once inside her house, she took a deep breath and let it out, allowing the tension to go with it. She put her notebook on the table and took the jam and bread out of her shopping bag.

"It was all a mistake."

This time, Janet's voice spoke the words, and Helen twisted around to find the source. The sudden motion threw her off balance, and she fell, grabbing at the kitchen counter on her way to the carpeted floor where she landed on her right shoulder. The impact emptied her lungs of air and, for a few seconds, she couldn't breathe.

FIVE

When her breath returned, the pain almost took it away again. As carefully as she could, she rolled onto her back, her shoulder and arm in such agony that she worried she might pass out. The thought that passing out might not be so bad, that, in fact, dying would be all right, flitted through her mind. She pushed it away. She'd just lie there for a little while until she felt better.

She hoped she hadn't broken anything. She couldn't be laid up. That's how people her age wound up dead. She had to keep moving. Immobility killed. She didn't think she could avoid the doctor this time if she'd fractured a bone — or bones.

After a while, the pain eased somewhat, and that was encouraging. But it wouldn't be easy getting off the floor. She had enough trouble rising from a chair. She tried rolling over to the left so she could use her left arm to push herself to her knees, but intense pain ripping through her shoulder stymied that effort. She decided to wait a little longer. She needed to get up, if only to reach the telephone. Otherwise, she might die right there.

Eventually, she settled on a plan. She would use the nearest chair at the dining room table to pull herself up without disturbing her right arm too much. She'd do it all with her left arm. But first, she had to get to the chair, which was about six feet away and on the wrong side of her body. She would need to turn herself 180 degrees. On the carpet, it wouldn't be easy.

She reached out with her left arm and tried to grasp a handful of carpet to pull herself around. She couldn't hold on because the nap was too low. The threads slipped from her fingers. She would have to use her lower body to wriggle herself into a position where she could grab a leg to pull the chair closer.

Keeping her upper body as still as possible to avoid aggravating her shoulder, she shifted her hips toward the chair and then moved her legs in the same direction. She didn't make much progress, but it was progress nevertheless. With frequent rests, she managed to rotate herself clockwise and bring her body closer to the chair at the same time.

Besides the injured shoulder, she had her arthritis to contend with. Her back, hips, knees and ankles ached all the time anyway. This awkward scuttle made the discomfort many times worse.

After what seemed like hours, she lay within three feet of the chair. She thought she could, at least for a moment, stop to rest.

Lying there, breathing heavily, she wasn't sure she was up to the task ahead. She took hold of the chair leg and pulled it toward her. Luckily, the furniture was fairly lightweight, and it moved without a lot of effort. She positioned the chair with the seat toward her.

Exhausted, she lay still, trying to recover her strength. But now she needed to go to the bathroom. It was quickly getting to the point of urgency.

Grabbing the chair leg again with her left hand, she tried to pull herself onto her left side so she wouldn't put weight on her hurt shoulder. Immediately, she realized she couldn't get the leverage she needed to stand up. Breathing slowly and deeply to control her growing desperation, she lay motionless, thinking. She had to raise herself to a sitting position so she could use the chair as support to climb to her feet.

She hauled the chair toward her head and grasped the edge of the seat. Then she dragged her feet up so her knees were elevated and, holding her right shoulder as still as possible, pushed with her feet and pulled with her left arm.

What seemed like a long time later but couldn't have been more than a minute, she was sitting up, her legs stretched out, wanting to cry with both relief and pain. She needed to rest, but she didn't have time. Her bladder couldn't hold out much longer.

Using her left hand on the chair to assist, she rocked on her buttocks until she could turn over onto her stomach. This action required that she release her grip on the chair seat, which trapped her left arm under her body and jarred her right shoulder. She almost screamed but held it in. Struggling to get her left arm free intensified the pain, but she finally succeeded.

Now her left arm was on the wrong side of her body. She would need to turn 90 degrees to reach the seat. That would mean getting to her knees.

She wished she'd been more faithful about doing the exercises her oldest son had taught her. She hated the workouts, but maybe they would have given her a little more strength. It didn't matter. She hadn't done them, so she had no one to blame but herself for the pickle she was in.

The left side of her face now rested on the carpet, and she could see how lousy a housekeeper she was. A vacuuming was long overdue, and dust made the baseboards look furry. Fine. She'd do better when she recovered. Getting up was all she should focus on right now.

She planted her left hand flat on the floor and tried to raise her upper body, managing to lift herself only a couple of inches. Getting herself up on her knees that way wouldn't work. So she decided to try it from the other end.

Her shoulder hurt so much that the temptation to just give up and wait for the sheriff to find her decomposing body was almost too powerful to resist. Not so long ago, she could have regained her feet with little trouble.

A year after she moved to Valley View, while she was birding with her youngest son, Tony, she'd nearly killed herself. She spotted what she thought was a canyon wren on a steep, rocky hillside and climbed up to get a closer look. She trained her binoculars on the area where she'd last seen the bird, and it flew. Taking a step backward to follow its flight up the hill, she rolled on loose rock and fell about six feet straight down.

Her son saw the accident and ran up the hill, kneeling at her side. He touched her face and then, being a physician, checked the pulse at her neck. She opened her eyes.

"I'm not dead."

Tony removed his fingers from her neck. "No, you're not. Are you okay?"

"Something's wrong with my arm."

Tony shifted position so he could examine his mother's left arm. It rested close to her side on a rounded stone half buried in the hillside, lying at an odd angle, drooped over the stone as if the bone connecting the shoulder and the elbow were made of rubber.

She winced when Tony touched the affected area. "Your humerus is broken. We'll need to call an ambulance so we can stabilize it and get you to the hospital. I'll need to drive back to the house to use the phone. Will you be all right here for a little while?"

"Don't be silly." She reached over her body, took hold of her left arm near the wrist and, gritting her teeth so she wouldn't cry out, pulled it across her body so her left hand rested on her belly.

"Help me get up."

Tony knelt at her head and reached under her, his hands between her shoulder blades. "Are you sure you want to do this?"

She nodded. He lifted her as she strained to pull herself into a sitting position. The pain wasn't as bad as she thought it would be, but it hurt enough to wrench a groan from her.

Once she was sitting up, still holding her left hand to her belly, she took a breath.

"Okay. Now help me stand up."

"We really should stabilize that break."

"It's stable enough."

Still, Tony hesitated.

She glared at him. "Look, I'm going to walk down that hill and get in the car. Then you're going to drive me to the hospital."

"That's not a good idea."

"I don't care."

Tony shook his head but stood and moved to squat at her right side. Placing his left hand under her right arm and his right in the small of her back, he pulled and pushed until she could get her legs under her and stand. It felt like someone was trying to twist her arm off just below the shoulder. This time, the pain brought both a groan and tears. Her knees growing weak, she leaned against Tony, determined not to pass out and fall again.

"Do you want to sit down?"

The thought of trying to get up again nauseated her. "Let's just go."

It took more than 10 minutes to make the 100-foot walk to the base of the hill and another 10 minutes to shuffle the 200 feet to the car. All the way, she leaned against Tony and held her left arm as tightly as she could to her side. Agony and fear of passing out and falling accompanied each step.

Somehow, with Tony's help, she managed to clamber into the Blazer. Tony hurried to take the wheel and drove her 50 miles to the nearest hospital.

Lying on the carpeted floor of her cabin, she wished Tony, with his young, strong arms, were with her now. But she'd wanted to make it on her own out here, and now she had to accept the consequences.

Once more, she tried to raise her upper body off the floor using only her left hand. This time, she managed to get enough leverage to raise her body to the point where she could pull her left leg up so her knee rested under her. Now she could allow some of her weight to rest on that knee as she drew her right leg forward and let her right knee take its place next to her left. From there, she could push herself upright. On her knees, she sidled a little closer to the chair and used the seat to help her stand.

A wave of vertigo almost sent her to the floor again, but she was able to turn and sit down hard on the chair. The jolt sent a bolt of torment through her entire right side. In response to the insult, she sobbed, letting her tears flow and finding that they seemed to wash away a little of the pain.

Somehow, she'd held her urine through the entire ordeal, but she couldn't any longer. She had to make it to the bathroom. Wiping her tears away, she stood up slowly because she feared both falling again and aggravating her pain. For a few seconds, she held on to the back of the chair. The room spun but then steadied, and she was able to make it through the kitchen to the bathroom, weaving only a little. Even with an elastic waistband, pulling her pants down proved a bit of a struggle, and she was afraid she might lose control with victory so near. Finally, she pushed her pants below her knees. She was able to yank her panties down and drop to the toilet seat, inciting another spasm of intense pain that left her gasping, but the relief that came with emptying her bladder almost made up for it.

She didn't know how badly she'd hurt herself, whether she'd broken any bones or only suffered bruising. Either way, she decided not to tell anyone what had happened. Falling like she had could mean a one-way trip to a home, and she certainly wasn't ready for that. No, best keep it to herself.

Right now, though, she needed to stand up. Supporting her right arm with her left hand, she leaned forward and tried to use her legs to push herself upright. It didn't work. The toilet was too low. Her second-eldest son Harvey had suggested, a few years ago, that she replace the old commode with a higher one, but she'd pooh-poohed the idea. Then he bought her a riser, but she left it sitting beside the toilet, unused. Now she was afraid she'd be left marooned on the stool.

What she needed was momentum, so she began rocking. The motion brought enough pain to force a groan and tears, but she persisted until she thought a forward thrust would be enough to allow her legs to take over the burden. Her buttocks rose from the toilet seat, and her knees almost buckled, but she came to her feet — and almost fell into the bathtub. Her panties and pants trapped her legs, and she staggered a couple of short steps before she regained her balance.

Now she faced a dilemma. In her hurry to get off the toilet, she'd forgotten to pull her underwear and pants up so she could reach them from a standing position without bending over and risking a world of hurt from her right shoulder. So should she let her pants and underwear slip to the floor so she could free her legs? Or should she try walking back to the living room, where a chair of sufficient height waited, and take the chance of being tripped by her own restricting clothing? Keeping her panties and pants just below her knees would make it easier to reach them with one hand from a sitting position. She could then pull them up higher and stand to finish the job.

She almost opted to let them drop to the floor so she could step out of them. Getting to the dining room chair seemed a long and hazardous journey with clothing binding her legs. With the garments gone, she could walk unfettered to her dresser for fresh panties and her closet for a clean pair of pants . . . except how would she put them on? No, she would just have to risk another fall.

Using her knees to exert enough outward pressure to keep her clothing up, she left the bathroom, taking tiny, shuffling steps, holding her right arm tight against her side with her left hand. She feared that letting go of her right arm would bring on such pain that she would fall to her knees, so she kept a firm grip on it. She couldn't risk freeing it to steady herself using the kitchen counter, so she shuffled through the kitchen, making progress in increments of inches.

By the time she reached the dining room chair, she felt weak with fatigue. She tried to sit slowly but dropped the last six inches and grunted as the shock brought renewed agony to her shoulder and arm.

The clock on the wall, a Christmas gift from her third son William, read almost 3:00. It had been nearly three hours since Janet's disembodied voice had knocked her off her feet. The clock, which used a picture of a songbird instead of a number for each hour, made a small mechanical clicking sound followed by the high-pitched, sweet song of an American goldfinch.

She closed her eyes and let the bird's song carry her back to spring mornings when she walked through the tall grass near the marsh she'd chosen as her study area. For a little while, her pain receded as she heard again not only the goldfinches but also the rusty-gate song of red-winged blackbirds and, of course, the rapid *kik-kik-kik* of the king rail. She could almost smell the rich, swampy odor.

She jerked awake. She had dozed off and relaxed the grip on her right arm. The arm had slipped off her thigh, causing an intense shock of pain. She grabbed her right wrist and pulled her arm back onto her thigh.

About 10 minutes later the pain had eased enough that she thought she could attempt pulling up her underwear and pants. The action would certainly increase her discomfort, but she couldn't put it off any longer. After all, she'd have to go to the bathroom again before long, and she wanted to take some aspirin and put ice on her wounded shoulder.

Pulling her right arm across her thighs, she winced but managed to get the limb into a position where it would stay put and free her left hand. Then she leaned forward and reached for her panties. The motion put pressure on her right arm, pulling it forward and down. She moaned and decided she didn't want to do it again to reach her pants. So she grabbed the top of both garments and pulled them up over her thighs. They slid over her skin with little resistance, and she sighed with relief.

Now she'd need to stand while holding on to her clothing so it wouldn't fall down again. She got to her feet as slowly as she could, letting her right arm slide off her lap, with predictable consequences.

When she could breathe and open her eyes again, she slowly pulled her underwear and pants up, being careful not to let her right arm move. Tempted to sit down again, she fought the urge and instead held her right arm still with her left hand and walked to the bathroom, where she let the arm go, opened the medicine cabinet and removed a bottle of aspirin. Using her teeth to hold the cap still, she turned the bottle until it opened. Then she tucked the bottle into her waistband, grabbed her right arm to stabilize it and returned to the kitchen, where she removed the open bottle from her pants and shook about 10 aspirin tablets onto the counter.

She almost used the cap in her mouth to close the aspirin bottle but thought better of it. She might need more tablets. Why close off the supply? Letting the cap fall into her hand, she placed it next to the bottle, filled a glass she kept near the sink with water and took four aspirins. Too many, but she was pretty sure it wouldn't be enough.

From the freezer, she retrieved a bag of crushed ice left over from the last time her fourth son Paul visited, arriving alone because he and Rebecca had decided on a "trial separation," which meant their marriage was over at long last.

She dropped the bag on the counter to break up the ice and spread a dish towel near it. Taking the twist tie off the bag with one arthritic hand proved frustrating, but she accomplished the task and dropped chunks of ice into a smaller plastic bag before wrapping that bag in the towel to form a compress. She pressed it against her shoulder as she made her way to her recliner.

In the chair, she leaned backward and let her body weight do the work. Soon, she was almost flat on her back, her feet supported by the footrest. She would worry about getting back up when the time came. For now, she just wanted to rest and let the aspirin and ice give her some relief.

She and Ed had been married 45 years when he died. Born a Lutheran, she converted to Catholicism to marry him. Her mother had not been happy with her decision, but it bothered her not at all. Religion to her was a necessity, given her place in society. She was the daughter of a physician and would be the wife of a physician, and certain things were expected of her. Belonging to a religious sect was one of those things. So she went along with expectations. She frankly didn't see much difference between Lutherans and Catholics, except in the ceremonies. She knew about Martin Luther and his problems with the Church, but they seemed rather petty. What she knew about Catholics was that they frowned on marrying outside the Church. Changing was easy. After all, she wasn't abandoning her religion.

The Catholic Church also disapproved of divorce or, more to the point, remarriage. You could get a divorce — that was a civil matter — but you couldn't marry anyone else unless you were able to get a Church-sanctioned annulment. Three of her sons had been divorced at least once. They didn't try to get an annulment. Instead, they quit the Church, a decision that seemed quite easy for them. They appeared unconcerned about the hellfire awaiting them.

She figured the next time she saw Paul he'd be divorced. He and Rebecca would share custody of their son Andrew, and they'd go about their lives, like millions of other divorced people, until they found someone new. It was the way things happened these days.

She hoped the hellfire thing was no more than a Catholic quirk and the Church had found some way to accommodate the changing attitude. She hadn't kept up with the rule changes, except she knew eating meat on Friday no longer damned Catholics to perdition. Nowadays, it was simply a recommendation. Funny how even the most hard-and-fast rules could change with the times. She wasn't sure it was a good thing, but it certainly did happen.

The ice and aspirin, along with lying still, seemed to be helping. She closed her eyes, thinking she might take a little nap.

"It was all a mistake."

This time, it was a trio of voices, Ed, Janet, Robert Beekman, singing rather than speaking, and repeating the line over and over. But she didn't let them scare her into reacting the way she had before. Instead, she opened her eyes and tried to locate the source. It seemed to be outside the house, in the front yard, like carolers at Christmas.

She wanted to get up and confront these people, but she had to rest. She closed her eyes and tried to shut out the chorus. Eventually, it faded away, and she fell asleep.

When she awoke, the ice compress had slipped off her shoulder and onto the arm of the chair. It was just as well. She didn't want to overdo it with the cold.

A glance at the clock told her she'd been sleeping for almost two hours, but she was in no hurry to get out of the chair. Her shoulder hurt, and the rest of her body felt as though she'd been beaten. Every joint in her left arm protested loudly when she tried to lift it. She knew the same would be true of her legs.

In the end, it didn't matter how badly she wanted to stay put. She couldn't. The bathroom beckoned.

Her right forearm rested across her belly, so all she had to do was hold it as still as possible with her left hand and lean forward until the recliner's footrest folded under the chair and she could stand. She raised her head and immediately regretted it as the dull ache already present in her neck magnified instantly to a piercing stab, as though someone had cranked the pain volume from low to ear-drum bursting. She groaned as she let her head fall back. She would have to hold her head in one position, rising like Dracula from his coffin in the old movies. It wouldn't be easy.

Once again, she raised her head, this time more from the waist, trying to maintain a straight line from her hips to the top of her head. This maneuver reduced the pain enough to make it bearable. It also shifted her weight so the chair back began to rise and the footrest to fall.

It had been some time since she'd used her stomach muscles this way, and she felt the strain. But she continued to rise until her feet were on the floor, feeling some pride in her accomplishment. She almost wished her worry-wart kids were there to see what she could do.

Wriggling forward enough to stand up while keeping her head still and back straight proved so painful that she had to take it an inch at a time. When she finally sat on the edge of her chair, ready to get to her feet, exhaustion made her weak and shaky.

After giving herself a minute to rest, she rose and stood, her legs quivering and nearly buckling but holding her upright. Still grasping her right arm, bracing it tightly against her body, she walked with tiny shuffling steps to the bathroom, proud that she staggered only once on the way. This time, she would use the riser. She had injured herself, after all. She'd have to make accommodations for a little while. With some difficulty, she retrieved the riser from where it leaned against the wall and positioned it on the stool.

On her way back to the living room after urinating, she stopped to take three more aspirin. She thought about retrieving the ice compress and refilling it but decided against it. She wasn't sure she could carry it and keep her right arm supported. Maybe she could rig a sling and free up her left arm and hand. But that meant a lot of pain and too much frustration as she tried to fold, tie and then put the sling on — not to mention adjust it to fit right. She took a fourth aspirin and shuffled back to the recliner, easing herself into it and leaning back as slowly as she could. Using the remote, she turned the television on and stared at the flickering screen until she fell asleep.

She woke to find that her right arm had slipped off her belly and lay in the space between her body and the chair arm. The room had grown dark, so, whimpering, she reached for the lamp that sat on the table beside her and switched it on. She could see that her forearm had turned black and blue all the way to her hand. The dark mottling scared her. Using her good hand, she lifted her right arm and placed it back on her belly. Repositioning helped ease the pain a little, but she would need more aspirin and the cold compress. And, of course, she had to go to the bathroom again.

Using the same strategy she'd employed before, she managed to get out of the chair and make her way to the bathroom. Returning to the kitchen, she realized she was hungry and took it as a good sign. But preparing food with one hand would be difficult, if not impossible. She decided she'd have to rig some way to support her right arm besides holding it up with her left hand.

Resting her right forearm on the counter, she opened a drawer full of dish towels and pulled out the biggest one she could find. Laying the towel on the counter and using only her left hand, she folded it into a triangle.

Now came the hard part. Keeping her right arm as still as possible, she manipulated the folded towel so she could grasp one end with her right hand. It hurt, but the pain was manageable. Then, using both hands, with the other end of the towel in her left, she tied the ends of the triangle's long side together. It took three tries, but she finally succeeded. Using her left hand and her teeth, she pulled the knot tight. Then it was simply a matter of draping the crude sling around her neck and sliding it under her arm. The result wasn't perfect, but it would do. This time, she took only two aspirin. The cold compress could wait until she'd had something to eat.

She used her ancient electric opener to take the lid off a can of chicken noodle soup and had that for dinner, sitting at the dining table with her notebook and binoculars for company. It felt good to return to some kind of normalcy, even though it had been only a few hours since the accident. Her entire body still hurt, and she expected this level of pain would continue for a couple of days. In the meantime, she would sleep in the recliner with the aspirin and a glass of water within easy reach.

This had been an unusual day. If tomorrow were similar, it would likely kill her. She blew on a spoonful of hot soup and thought about the new bird, hoping it would come back.

SIX

After a fitful night in the recliner, she woke to the muffled roar of Piñon Creek. Pain and the need to use the bathroom roused her this time, not the voices.

She attempted to stand but found that, no matter what part of her body she moved, it hurt. Lying back, she waited a few minutes, then tried to work the pain out by rolling her left shoulder — leaving the right one alone — and turning her head and legs to ease the stiffness in her muscles and joints. When she thought she could, she attempted to get out of the chair and, with a groan and a few whimpers, succeeded. When she stood, her knees threatened to buckle, so she sat back down on the edge of the seat until her strength returned.

When she stood again, her ability to remain upright pleased her. One tentative step followed another until she reached the bathroom. On the way back, still stepping carefully, she stopped at the kitchen sink, filled a glass with water and took two aspirin. Then she walked slowly to the dining table and sat. Beyond the windows, early light revealed her collection of feeders and the steep, rocky slope across the creek. The first birds of the day were already at their places, pecking at seeds and suet. She noted that some of the tube feeders were low on seed and wondered how long it would be before she could get out to fill them.

From the same river birch as it had emerged yesterday, the new bird flew to one of the thistle seed tubes and began feeding. She picked up her binoculars with her left hand and held them to her eyes, excited and pleased to see the bird again and wishing she hadn't hurt herself.

She didn't dare leave the house in her current condition. If anyone saw her sling and black-and-blue arm, they'd insist she see a doctor, and she'd have to explain how the accident happened. She could make up a story about tripping over a root while walking in the woods or something, but she wasn't good at lying. Someone might call one of her sons, and the whole thing could be blown out of proportion. No, she'd just lie low for a little while until the bruising cleared up or she could wear long sleeves without the sling. Thank God she had gone to the store and picked up more bread and strawberry jam.

She put the binoculars down and stood up, resting her left hand on the table just a moment for support, and walked carefully to the kitchen where she made her usual breakfast. When she had prepared the toast and made her cup of instant coffee, she carried the items, one at a time, to the table. The first sip of coffee tasted better than ever, and the toast with jam rivaled the croissants from the Double Dyke Bakery.

Wanting to savor her meal, she put the toast down and picked up the binoculars again. The new bird remained at the thistle seed feeder. Two mountain chickadees and a white-breasted nuthatch occupied a suet feeder. The black-billed magpie and the Steller's jay played out their daily combat at a platform feeder, and the dark-eyed juncos pecked at seeds on the ground, each of them minding its own business. She wanted to write down what she saw, but she was right-handed, and she couldn't use that hand. For a little while, she'd just have to trust her memory and catch up with her lists when she could use a pen again.

She put the binoculars down and took a sip of coffee and another bite of toast, watching the birds behave the way they always did. She appreciated the predictability of it.

When things didn't go the way she expected, nothing good came of it. Her fall the day before served as a good example. So did her ornithology professor's criticism. That sudden betrayal had left her miserable for months, even after he gave her a high grade for her work. And "betrayal" was the only word that fit.

Even though Beekman was quite a lot younger, she'd seen him as a mentor. That he would turn on her in the way he had seemed completely uncalled for and cruel. She'd done nothing to deserve it, except take his course out of interest in the subject, not to earn a doctorate and become a professor herself. She had no such ambition. She simply wanted more out of life than being a wife and mother, and birds gave her the opportunity.

After all these years, the anger remained fresh, as if the affront had happened yesterday. She felt the sting of tears and fought them back, loathe to let that man get to her again. But she still felt it in her chest — insult added to injury, emotional hurt creating the physical discomfort.

Hoping the aspirin would start to do its work soon, she took another sip of coffee and returned her attention to the new bird who clung to the perch on the thistle seed feeder and created a shower of black seed hulls as it fed. Her coffee had gone cold, so she returned to the kitchen to make another cup.

The act of getting up and taking the first step brought pain, but she'd learned to expect that on the best of days. She was sure movement would ease it, at least a little. By the time she reached for the tea kettle, she was able to move more easily, and the return trip to the table was almost bearable.

Seated again, she rested her right arm on the table and removed the sling to get a better look at it. She had been avoiding the sight all morning and was reluctant to confront it now. But look she did, and what she saw made her ill. The entire limb was mottled black and blue with some green mixed in for effect. On the positive side, it didn't appear much worse than it had the night before. She decided to take that as a good sign and put the sling back on.

Eventually, the pain would be less, although it would probably never go away entirely. Experience had taught her that injuries left permanent reminders — persistent aches, sensitivity to weather changes and other annoyances. This one was sure to mete out punishment for her carelessness until the day she died. Until then, at least it would let her know she was still alive.

Her toast was cold, but it still tasted good. So she focused on her food, alternating bites of toast and sips of coffee until both were gone. While she was eating, the aspirin took effect, and she felt much better.

Driving would be out of the question until she could use her arm again to lift herself into the Blazer, but maybe she could do some laundry to keep herself busy. And there were always the birds to watch and study. She'd be fine for a few days. Sometimes, in the winter, she wouldn't leave the house or see anyone for weeks, relying on the television to keep in touch with what was going on in the world. Not that she cared, particularly, but it seemed wise to stay as up to date and stimulated as possible. Otherwise, she might sink, as her mother had, into the quicksand of dementia.

Her mother, Olga Svenson before she married, was a child of Swedish immigrants. She did her best to raise two sons and a daughter to be good Lutherans and to know their place, as the children of a physician, in their small-town society. When the son of Irish Catholic parents came along and expressed an interest in marrying Olga's only daughter, the proposal did not sit well. The fact that the suitor aspired to become, and did become a physician made little difference. He remained outside the young woman's social class.

Olga's husband, John Harker, came from British stock and was also a Lutheran. But he didn't seem to care that his soon-to-be son in law was a papist. Olga let it be known that the circumstances and her husband's apparently lackadaisical attitude toward the situation, were not to her liking. To her frustration, her dissatisfaction mattered not a whit. The wedding came and went, and Olga made the best of it because to do anything else would be unseemly.

Over the years, as Ed finished medical school, she warmed to him somewhat, although his papism and Irish roots continued to bother her. She even seemed to worry for him a little when he decided to join the Navy. He served and never saw action, but the possibility of losing him was a constant presence.

After Ed's stint in the service, he and Helen settled in a town only about 100 miles from John and Olga's home. Her dad died 10 years before Ed, and her mother seemed to shut the world out. She'd always been somewhat standoffish, but she made sure to perform her social duties, if not enjoy them. After her husband died, she apparently decided that the social niceties were no longer required, and she took to sleeping on the living room sofa most of the day. On more than one occasion, Helen and Ed had paid a visit and found her mother lying there. Sometimes, she seemed to have trouble deciding who they were, and Ed thought maybe it was time for her to move to a place where she could be cared for.

They settled on a nursing home in their town just a few blocks from their home. By that time, Olga only sometimes recognized people she'd known well. Two years later, she died.

Recalling her parents' life and death, Helen realized how intensely she had loved her father, a sweet, gentle, and necessarily patient man. Her mother she had never liked, even before Olga treated Ed like some kind of lowlife. Her father had spent much of his free time in the basement, doing woodworking projects while she and her brothers played with the toys their father made. It dawned on her now why he didn't want to go upstairs. Although he always treated his wife with respect and kindness, he preferred not to be around her.

Helen remembered that, throughout her childhood and adolescence, her mother rarely left the house. The world beyond her door seemed to frighten her. So her home became the center of social activity. Women came for coffee and tea, to play bridge and to plan events. The place was busy, but Olga stayed aloof, letting other people take control while she sat off to one side, allowing the women to approach her but seldom, if ever, making the first move. She had a maid to greet her guests and serve refreshments. John made it a point to be away seeing patients or in the basement doing his woodworking and keeping the children quiet.

Looking back, she understood that her parents' marriage was at best one-sided, as far as affection was concerned. Her father seemed to love his wife, but for her, it was a union based on status and obligation. She would bear his children because good wives did that. She would perform the social niceties because that was her job. But she did not enjoy his company, or at least she never revealed her pleasure. Her smiles, when they came, opened a fissure in her face like a crack in arctic ice. Anyway, that was the way Helen remembered it. It was a long time ago, after all.

She'd drifted off again, letting memories take her to a place she didn't want to go, a journey that left her feeling sad and angry.

"It was all a mistake."

This time it was her mother's voice. It sounded angry. And sorrowful. The anger she recognized. The sorrow she'd never experienced before, and it frightened her. She stood and held on to the table, her unsteadiness caused more by the unfamiliar emotion in her mother's voice than any physical infirmity. She turned and half-sat on the edge of the table, trying to clear her head and find the source of the words she had come to know and hope never to hear again.

Every time she heard the voices, she forgot, for a time, that they came from inside her own head. They sounded so real, so intimate that she reacted as she would if the people the voices belonged to were with her. Each time, she felt a shiver, and the muscles in her shoulders and back contracted as if to ward off an attack. But these were people she had known and even loved. Why did she react the way she did? What was there to fear?

Whatever the mistake was, she now believed it wasn't something she had done. It seemed less an accusation than a confession. The mistake had been theirs, not hers, and they were telling that truth. Or maybe she was just spending too much time alone and was a little stir-crazy. She needed to hear the sound of her own voice.

"What was your mistake?" Her words seemed to echo, as though spoken in a large, empty chamber. "What do you mean by 'all?'"

She waited, half expecting an answer from one or more of the figments of her imagination, but nothing happened. Speaking, though, seemed to break the spell, reassert her control over the situation and renew her confidence.

She sat down, picked up her binoculars and scanned the yard. The new bird was gone, leaving an assembly of magpies, jays, nuthatches, chickadees and juncos. She put the binoculars down, a little harder than necessary.

"Hell's bells." It was as close as she came to swearing, except for the occasional "Damn" and, once, a long time ago during a moment of extreme frustration, "Shit."

Now Ed could swear, and he didn't care whether the children were present to hear it. In that way and a number of others, he was very different from her father. John never swore, and he wouldn't use the word "God," believing no one was worthy of such presumption. For Ed, on the other hand, "God damn son of a bitch" came as naturally as "How are you?" It was his foundational curse, something on which to build a temple to profanity if he felt it was called for.

Once, at her urging, he attempted to quit using words he wouldn't tolerate from his children. He did try, for a while, substituting "Oh, bugs" for the language he was more comfortable with. It didn't work. "God damn son of a bitch" returned, its power too difficult to overcome, like smoking. She gave up. In the end, the kids seemed no worse for the lessons in objectionable language.

She had to admit she missed the streaks of profanity. They even seemed tame now. These days, "fuck" had become the new "God damn," and she saw that as a step in the wrong direction. Since when did the sex act, no matter what term is used for it, become a preferred swear word?

She took the time once to look up the etymology of "fuck." Following its trail led her to decide that its use under a wide variety of circumstances was the result of its having no distinctive meaning. It could refer to the sex act, of course, but also indicate abrupt dismissal — "Fuck off" — frustration — "Ah, fuck it" — mismanagement — "All fucked up" — and other situations and emotions. As an adjective, it was all-purpose: "That's fucking awful," "That's fucking great," "We're in it all the fucking way." In other words, it could be used in almost any sentence and as any part of speech, as a kind of verbal reinforcement. The only thing missing by leaving it out would be a little enthusiasm.

She'd done it again, drifted off on a tangent. Maybe one day she'd get lost there. Watching her mother lose touch from day to day was painful as it was happening, but she didn't connect Olga's downward spiral and her own possible future at the time. Her mother was only 12 years older when she died than Helen was now, and she hadn't been able to care for herself for years before that.

Only 12 years. Olga had been dead far longer than that. She'd died five years before Ed.

"Hell's fucking bells." Saying the word out loud made her a little sick, but it also helped her feel younger. Ed would definitely not have approved. Her mother would have to spend a day or so on the fainting couch. Depending on how old she was when she said it, her father would have banished her to her room to contemplate her sin or looked terribly disappointed.

"Hell's fucking bells." It felt good to say it again. She might make it a regular practice, as long as no one else could hear.

When she first noticed the knocking, she confused it with the sharp pounding of a hammer and wondered why someone would be working in her yard. She hadn't hired anyone. Then she realized the rapping was too rapid for hammer blows, that someone was at her back door. She turned to look, and Janet waved at her through the glass. She got up as quickly as she could and opened the door. The shock on Janet's face when she saw Helen's arm in the sling was almost funny.

"What . . .?

"Don't worry. I'm fine."

"That doesn't look fine."

"I just bruised it tripping over a root in the woods. It's nothing a little ice and aspirin won't take care of."

"Shouldn't you see a doctor? That must hurt."

"A little, but not enough to drive fifty miles. Anyway, a doctor will just tell me to ice up and take aspirin."

"You really should have that looked at."

"If I need help, I'll get it."

"Okay, okay. I'm just a little concerned."

"Well, come in, then, and drop the subject. Want some coffee?"

"Sure."

Janet took a seat at the table with her back to the feeder array as Helen cleared her dishes and placed her plate in the sink and her mug on the counter next to the stove. She pulled another mug out of the cupboard and put the tea kettle on to heat. Janet sat quietly but seemed to want to say something.

"If you're going to start in on me again about seeing a doctor, you can leave."

"No, no. I wouldn't want to cross you."

"Then what is it?"

Janet hesitated. "Did I hear you say, 'Hell's effing bells' a minute ago?"

She decided two lies in one morning would be too risky. "I didn't say hell's effing bells. I said hell's fucking bells. And if you tell a single soul what you heard, I'll never speak to you again. Is that clear?"

"Absolutely."

"Let's talk about something else."

"All right. But . . ."

Helen gave Janet her best don't-go-there look. It did the job.

"Okey, dokey. It's none of my business anyway."

Helen spooned some instant coffee into her mug and Janet's. "You're right there."

"You know, you don't have to drink that freeze-dried stuff. You can pick up a bag of fresh-ground at the Double Dyke."

"I like the freeze-dried stuff. Anyway, I don't have a coffeemaker."

"Okay."

The kettle began to whistle. Helen took it off the burner and poured water into the two mugs.

"Do you want milk or sugar?"

"Please. Lots of both."

"Right." She put two spoons of sugar in Janet's mug and got the milk from the refrigerator, adding a generous helping to Janet's coffee.

"You can carry your own to the table."

"Of course." Janet jumped from her seat and walked quickly to the kitchen, returning to her chair, coffee in hand.

Helen followed Janet to the table, sat and sipped her coffee. "Why are you here?"

The question seemed to catch Janet by surprise. "I just wanted to say hi."

"You're checking on me."

"Well, yes. I was a little worried. You seemed distracted yesterday. I wanted to be sure everything's all right."

"Everything's fine. My marbles remain in place."

Janet took a sip of her coffee and winced. Her attempt to cover the expression with a bright smile failed. "Perfect."

"Uh, huh." Helen pointed at Janet's mug. "I won't be offended if you bring your own next time."

"No, it's good. Really."

Janet turned around to check the birdfeeders. She pointed and looked over her shoulder at Helen. "What's that?"

The new bird was back on the thistle seed feeder. Helen picked up her binoculars and handed them to Janet. "It's the new one. Take a look while I go to the bathroom."

Janet raised the binoculars and clumsily worked the focus nob. Helen took advantage of Janet's attention on the bird to stand, grimacing. She walked to the bathroom and shut the door behind her.

When she emerged, Janet's gaze remained fixed on the bird. "I'm not a birdwatcher," she said, "but I've never seen one like that before."

"It might be a new species."

Janet lowered the binoculars and turned around, her eyes wide. "You're kidding."

"No. I think this is a completely new bird. At least new to science."

"At your feeder?"

"At my feeder. It eats for a while and then flies up toward the campground, following the creek. I think there might be more of them up there somewhere."

Janet grinned. "This is a big story."

"No, it isn't." Helen's don't-go-there look operated at full power, and Janet sat back.

"But . . ."

"No. Not yet. I have to be absolutely certain. A specimen would be ideal."

"You mean you'd kill it?"

"No. I wouldn't. But someone else will surely want to."

"Why? What do you need that you can't get from a live bird?"

"Live birds can tell us a lot. We can even determine if one belongs to a new species by looking at its DNA. But to really understand a species, you need what are called voucher specimens. They're preserved in different ways to document different features. That's why natural history museums keep them and add to them, so people can study them over time, use new techniques and look for things other scientists haven't considered."

"You seem to know a lot about this stuff."

"I learned it a long time ago. For a while I tried to keep up with the science, but I'd rather just watch the birds. I've written down a description. Now I need to send it to an expert."

"And who would that be?"

"Robert Beekman. He was my ornithology professor."

"Nice to have a personal connection."

"It's personal, I guess, but not pleasant."

"Bad blood between you?"

"You could say that. I thought he was a friend, but he changed."

"Do you trust him now?"

"I'm not sure, but he's the only expert I know."

Janet smiled. "Why don't you write out what you want to say, and I'll send your note and the description to Beekman by email? Better yet, let me photograph the bird, and we'll include the pictures."

Helen hesitated, staring at the new bird on the feeder. "Are you sure that's a good idea? From what I've heard, you can trust the U.S. Mail more than email."

"It'll be fine."

For a while, Helen said nothing, keeping her eyes on the new bird still feeding on thistle seed.

"No," she said.

"No what?"

"I don't want the evidence sent out that way."

"What way? By email?"

"This has to be kept completely confidential. I shouldn't have told you about it."

"Helen, the chances of someone — anyone — intercepting an email and stealing your 'evidence' are remote, at best."

"No, I'll trust the regular mail. Is there any way to send the note and pictures without using a computer?"

"I could put the photos on a thumb drive."

"Thumb drive?"

"It's a computer thing. But it stores the information so you can send it by snail mail, or better yet, FedEx or UPS. That way, you can get it to Beekman faster."

"Right." Helen thought for a moment. "No photos. Too risky. I just want to send the description. If that doesn't work, I'll give him photos."

Janet stood. "Okay, if you're sure. I'll go now. Call me when you're done with your note."

Helen hesitated, then said, "I need one more thing, if it's all right."

"Name it."

"It's my arm. I can't write."

Janet frowned. Helen took her expression as evidence that she was again concerned about the extent of the injury, but Janet said, "Just dictate it to me."

Helen found some old stationery, and she and Janet sat at the table. Her note contained no questions about Beekman's health, his family or how things were going for him, only that she had seen a bird she couldn't identify and thought he might be interested. Otherwise, it included the bird's anatomical features, as she had recorded them in her notebook, and her phone number. She signed it with her left hand, "Thank you. Helen Bryan."

Helen put the note in an envelope, sealed it and affixed a stamp. "Can you use your infernal machine to find Beekman's address and put this in the mail? I'm not sure where he is now."

"Sure." Janet took the envelope and tucked it into her jacket pocket. "I'll do it as soon as I get back to the office."

After Janet pulled the back door shut and waved through the window, the quiet settled in. Helen could feel its pressure, relieved only slightly by the creek's muted roar. It was odd how silence seemed to have weight, and the sensation was not pleasant. She felt it on her damaged shoulder like a hand pressing down, and it radiated into her chest, where it rested on her heart. She expected to hear a voice telling her it had all been a mistake, but no one spoke.

"Hell's bells. Hell's fucking bells."

She stared at the new bird as it scattered the hulls of thistle seed from the feeder. A couple of minutes later, the sound of Janet's car engine starting snapped her out of her reverie, and she wondered, briefly, what had taken Janet so long to get going. Then again, Janet had told her the old car was unreliable. Her thoughts soon returned to the new bird and speculation about how Beekman would react.

As she saw it, there were two possibilities. He might be intrigued enough that he'd want to see the bird for himself. Or he could just throw the note away, dismissing it as an amateur's failure to recognize a hybrid, perhaps. She'd read recently about a cross between a white-throated sparrow and a golden-crowned sparrow. Both species could be found in Colorado, although the golden-crowned occurred rarely.

The pain in her arm and shoulder returned. She watched as the new bird flew away from the feeders and north, following the creek.

SEVEN

A few aspirin tablets and a cold compress had Helen feeling better when Janet returned early in the afternoon. She handed Helen a special delivery receipt.

"Thought you might like to know I really did send it," Janet said with a smile.

"Thank you." Helen took the receipt, saying nothing more about it.

"Car trouble?" she asked.

Janet seemed surprised by the question.

"It took a while to start when you left this morning. Everything okay?"

Janet smiled again. "The old thing's about to give up the ghost, I'm afraid. Sometimes, I get just a click when I turn the key. It can go on like that for a while. I'm sure at some point, a click will be all I get, if anything."

Janet's smile disappeared. A pensive look replaced it. "I know it's a little late to ask, but are you sure you want Beekman to be your expert?"

"It's been so long. I don't know anybody else. Would you like a cup of coffee?"

Janet shook her head a little too energetically. "I can't. I have to put this month's edition to bed. The printer needs it tomorrow."

When Janet left, the weight of the silence descended on Helen again. She sat at the table and picked up her binoculars.

The bird was back. Its magnified image convinced her it was something new and too important to let petty differences get in the way. She thought she knew Beekman well enough to trust his integrity as a scientist even if he was an asshole.

"Asshole" was like "fucking," a word she had never used before, only heard and read — and sometimes accidentally thought. It seemed appropriate under the circumstances, so she didn't mind thinking it and applying it to Beekman. The guy was a fucking asshole, no doubt about it. But she needed him. He was a damned good ornithologist. She had to have the backing of someone like him to make her case for a new species. Now she could only wait to hear from him.

She'd almost forgotten what it was like to be excited about anything.

But there it was, something like the feeling she'd had when she and Ed had sex the first time, a pleasant, though somewhat disturbing surge in her groin and the pit of her stomach when he touched her leg under her skirt and kissed her neck. He'd done those things before, but that night she knew what was going to happen.

She wanted it to happen, in spite of all the lectures from her mother about giving away her "sacred parts" to a man she wasn't married to. That night, she didn't give a damn about saving her "sacred parts" for marriage. She wanted to have sex. So she did.

It wasn't quite what she'd expected. No bells pealed. No fireworks filled the sky. But it was nice, although it did hurt a little. Afterward, she felt like she'd made the right decision. As Ed breathed deeply and evenly beside her, she smiled and closed her eyes, anxious to try sex again, sure it would be better and better with practice.

And it did get better, much better, at least until she and Ed got married and started having children. It became more and more difficult to find time for sex. What with a physician's schedule, Ed seemed less interested. By the time the fifth boy came along — almost 16 years after the first — she, too, had begun to see sex as more messy than exciting.

The change didn't happen suddenly. It was more a slow diminishing than a sudden shutting down, like a spigot being slowly turned off. She tried to dismiss it as a natural consequence of being together for so long and the exhaustion resulting from caring for children and working long hours, but it saddened her. She longed for the intensity of those first few years, when she and Ed could barely stand to be apart for a few hours and would fall into bed on the slightest pretense or no pretense at all, just mutual lust.

One thing that never crossed her mind was infidelity. She knew other women found Ed attractive. They told her so. And, although their lovemaking had become sporadic, it was anything but desultory when it did happen. Ed could still push all the right buttons, and he clearly enjoyed their time in bed.

All right, it crossed her mind, but she put it away in a dark space where she went only during the worst of times. One of those times came after her fourth boy was born. With the first three, she'd been able to get herself back in shape fairly quickly. She played tennis and worked in the garden until her body felt strong and as lithe as it would ever be.

After Paul, that all changed. She was over 40 by then. Losing weight and regaining muscle strength wasn't quite so easy. Calcium loss had affectted her bones and teeth, so she had to have extensive dental work. Looking at herself in the mirror became an act of courage because of her dimpled, wrinkled, sagging skin. Still, she kept up with her tennis and tending her garden, trying to bring back the woman she had once been.

Then, two years later, she had Tony. He was a surprise, of course, and, though she would never say it to him or Ed or anyone else, not a pleasant one. Paul, her fourth, had been a surprise, too. His arrival meant she'd be raising children for another 18 years. Now it would be 20 years. The idea of being past 60 before her children were all out of the nest left her dispirited.

It wasn't that she didn't love her children. She did. She just longed for some peace and quiet and time to pursue other interests, although she wasn't sure what those interests might be.

She had to admit that sometimes she thought of motherhood as a kind of factory job. Raising children was like working on a one-woman assembly line, putting the pieces in place as she ran back and forth from child to child, trying to keep up. It was exhausting and, often, discouraging. Not to mention unappreciated.

Ed worked hard, she knew, but he received both monetary and emotional rewards for his efforts. His patients loved him. Everyone else looked up to him. When he died, at 67, his funeral brought an overflow crowd. People stood outside on the church steps and the sidewalk. It looked like half the town showed up. It was small wonder he hadn't retired at 65 as she'd hoped he would. He kept on going until less than a year before he died, even though he probably shouldn't have been practicing anymore. The thought of losing all that respect and admiration must have been devastating.

She and Ed talked about retirement and even looked into buying a luxury RV so they could spend time in all the places they wanted to visit in North America and do it in comfort. But that idea faded within six months. Ed continued working, dedicating at least 14 hours a day to taking care of sick people. They stopped talking about retirement, and the subject didn't come up again until Ed seemed to be recovering somewhat from his stroke. At that point, the conversation had become one-sided.

Ed sat quietly, murmuring occasional assent, while she explained how they would transform the Valley View house from a primitive fishing cabin into a comfortable home in the woods. She hired a contractor and had plans drawn up for a complete renovation that would include the addition of a wheelchair ramp to the front door. She told Ed she wasn't sure the ramp would be necessary because, three months after the stroke, he was taking his first tentative steps with a cane, but she figured one of them, at least, would need that ramp at some point down the road.

Then came the day in December, only nine months after the stroke, when she and Ed were writing Christmas cards and he said he had a headache. Less than 24 hours later, he was dead.

After the funeral, alone in a house once filled with a husband and five kids, she had the peace and quiet she'd once longed for. She realized then what a huge space Ed had filled in her life, even before he became so dependent on her. The boys had been gone for a while now, the last having left for college five years earlier. She'd grown used to not having any of them underfoot anymore.

As big a part of her life as Ed had been, he could no longer make the house they'd shared a home. The silence lay heavy in every room. The bed seemed as vast as the Pacific Ocean where she and Ed had wandered the beaches in search of seabirds.

She occupied herself with the rituals of death, accepting food she would never eat and expressions of sympathy she found oddly annoying.

The contractor working on the house in Valley View called. He said he was sorry her husband died, but he needed to know if she planned to complete the project. If not, he'd bill her for the work he'd done.

Without hesitation, she told him to keep on working. She'd be moving in as soon as he was finished. The next day, she put the house she'd lived in for more than 30 years up for sale. It had become her albatross, and soon she'd be free of it. For the first time in a long time, she felt exhilarated.

Deciding what to keep and what to get rid of turned out to be less of an emotional challenge than she'd expected. She was moving from a 5,000-square-foot to a 900-square-foot house, so she had to let go of more stuff than she kept. Most of the large furniture had to go. She settled on the maple dining table and four chairs, the king-sized bed she and Ed had shared, a double bed for the spare bedroom, a matching sofa and love seat, the recliner and a few odds and ends to finish out the living room and spare bedroom. Ed's collection of family and bird photos made the cut, as did some of the books from his library and mementos from their years together. Otherwise, except for the washer and dryer, kitchen utensils, small appliances and dishes, almost everything went to auction, save the few items the boys gleaned.

Early on a March morning, one year and three months after Ed died, she drove the Blazer away from her home for the last time. She had nothing to come back for until they planted her in the Catholic cemetery next to her husband.

Her only regret that day was leaving her one real friend, Milly Brewster. Milly promised to visit her the first chance she got, and she did visit — three years later. That was the first and last time. They wrote to each other for a few years, mostly just Christmas and birthday cards, and then Milly got cancer and died without mentioning that she was sick.

Helen couldn't understand why Milly kept her illness a secret, and it angered her. Her anger served to take the edge off her grief, as did the lack of contact over a long period. She had trouble picturing Milly's face, so it didn't haunt her memory or her dreams. The friendship was a long chapter in her life, but it was over, and the last few pages had little to say.

When she arrived in Valley View, her house had already been set up. The beds, the dining table and chairs and the recliner were where she wanted them, thanks to Harvey, her second eldest, who oversaw the move. He had already left, returning to his own home in Montrose, about 160 miles west of

Valley View. He'd moved there with his wife and son 10 years earlier because he'd fallen in love with the mountains as a boy, thanks to the vacations in Valley View with his parents.

She didn't expect Harvey to come around very often, even though he was relatively close. He'd always been rather aloof around her. Like his father, he tended to show affection with a laugh, as if it were a joke. He seldom said, "I love you" to his children when they were young and never when they got older. He kept words like "love" for special occasions, somewhat embarrassed to say them, even to his wife.

She went along with Harvey's reticence, having adopted it herself from Ed. Hardly the hugger at any time, she preferred to keep a little distance between her and other bodies, except with Ed, and then only under certain circumstances, sex being pretty much the only circumstance. It was an arrangement that suited both of them and didn't seem to have any adverse effect on the boys. They all got plenty of lap-sitting time when they were small, and Ed carried each of them to the bathroom once a night to make sure they didn't wet the bed.

He'd sing "Zip-a-Dee-Doo-Dah" from *Song of the South* to every boy every night in a voice that would send anyone except a loving son away screaming for mercy. The kids seemed to love it.

In fact, the children adored their dad. Ed once told her he would never hit any of the boys because he was afraid he'd lose control and hurt them. She wasn't sure about that. She had a suspicion he just didn't want to be the disciplinarian. The task of punishing the kids' transgressions fell to her. That they preferred their father was a consequence, she figured, of absence and a hands-off approach to parenting.

It was understandable, she supposed. Ed's father — who insisted on being called Edward — wasn't shy about physical punishment. He had one solution for every behavioral problem — the belt — and he used it liberally. Helen would be the first to admit she was no psychologist, but she believed Edward's anger at his own lot in life came through in every crack of leather against flesh.

A traveling salesman peddling jams and jellies, Edward couldn't read and kept it a secret, managing to fake his way through life. Ed didn't know about his father's inability to read until Edward died and Ed's mother, Anne, broke the news.

Advances in the understanding of learning disabilities since Edward was born and raised told her he was probably dyslexic, but back then, everybody thought he was just stupid. Clearly, he wasn't, but he did grow up angry and ashamed. When he died, Ed inherited all the books his father had collected during his life, well over a thousand volumes from practically every genre. Helen sold them at the auction, having never read any of them. Ed hadn't read them, either, nor had the boys. Edward's legacy turned out to be a thousand unread books. Maybe they found someone to turn their pages after father and son were both gone.

Ed and his father were, unsurprisingly, not close. Ed held Edward responsible for the death of his little sister, Ruth, who died of scarlet fever when Ed was nine years old. As the story went, Edward didn't want to spend the money for a doctor and let the infection advance until it was too late to save the girl. Ed said it was amazing that the other children, all four of them, didn't get sick. He never forgave his father and refused to talk about the incident with him.

"Fucking asshole." At first, she thought someone else had said the words, but she quickly realized they'd come from her. She'd done it again, lost herself in memories she didn't want to recall. Using the table to help, she stood, weaved a bit and, when the vertigo eased, walked to the kitchen, where she filled the tea kettle, turned on a burner and placed the kettle on the coil.

Today, she would have toast and strawberry jam for lunch instead of breakfast. Sometimes it was good to step out of the routine and shake things up a bit. Compared to sending the photographs to Beekman, it was a small adventure with little risk, but it was wise not to take too many chances. Routine was the key to sanity, and she wanted to stay sane. She popped two pieces of bread in the toaster, pulled the jam out of the refrigerator and waited for the toast to emerge and the water to boil.

She stared out the window over the sink, watching the water in the creek tumble over rocks and pool behind the larger ones. Years ago, she had helped her sons fish for trout in this stream, even though she didn't care for fishing. She'd learned how from Milly and her husband Frank, who died a couple years before Ed. They took their trout fishing seriously and liked working the smaller streams like Piñon Creek. Unlike fly fishing, their method required stealth. They'd scout the stream for pools under banks or behind boulders and, staying out of sight of the fish, crawl up and drop a line in the water. For bait, they used earthworms. Their approach took patience, so the boys didn't like it right away. As they got older, though, they learned the rewards of taking their time.

But that was a long time ago. A lot of water had flowed by her house since she'd shown her last two boys how to fool the fish. Back then, she wouldn't have lost her balance and broken her arm or wrenched her shoulder. In those days, she didn't get dizzy when she stood up and, even if she did fall, she would have been able to get back on her feet right away. When she thought about how she had to struggle like a box turtle on its back, it made her furious.

She took several deep breaths, realizing how pointless it was to be so angry at something she could do nothing about. The kettle had started whistling, so she spooned some coffee into her mug and poured the boiling water over it. The toast was up, too. She followed her butter-and-jelly routine and carried the plate and mug to the table.

The new bird had gone. Its absence hit her harder than she would have expected. Would it come back? What if it didn't? She had the description, but she had no idea where the bird had come from. Surely there were more of its kind somewhere nearby. She should take a lesson from Milly and Frank and be patient. The bird had returned before. It would again. She took a bite of toast and sip of coffee and watched the juncos peck the dirt in search of seeds.

The phone rang, startling her so she spilled her coffee. She knew better than to try to hurry, and it rang six times before she got to it. She picked up the receiver, happy to cut off the jangle.

"Hello?"

"Hi, there. It's Ed."

She dropped the receiver, as if it were suddenly too hot to touch, and stared at it where it lay on the counter, her eyes wide with shock. She picked it up and held it a little distance from her ear.

"Mom? You there?"

It was Eddie, her eldest. She put the receiver to her ear and struggled to speak, finally rasping out, "You sound so much like . . ."

"Mom? You okay?"

"Yes, yes. I'm all right."

"You sure?"

"I'm fine. I was just thinking about your father, and I . . . Well, I guess I . . ."

"You've told me ever since I was a teenager that I sound like Dad. I'm sorry if I scared you."

"Don't worry about it. How is everybody?"

"We're fine. Are you feeling good?"

"As good as an eighty-five-year-old woman can. Are you afraid I'm going bonkers?"

"No, no, of course not. But you did give me a start there for a second."

She decided now would not be a good time to tell Eddie about her injury. It would just feed his worries. "How's work?"

He laughed. "Changing the subject, eh?"

"Yes."

"Well, work is work."

"That's helpful."

"I called to check on you, not to talk about me."

"Can't you do both? How are Meg, Jay, and Michael?"

Meg was Eddie's fourth wife. The boys were both born during his first marriage and were grownups with families of their own and still with their first wives. She didn't know why Eddie's three marriages failed, but the fact that he didn't want to discuss it was a clue. He'd probably been unfaithful.

"Meg's doing great. You know how she loves teaching."

"Yes, I do. Will she be retiring soon?"

"Mom, she's only thirty."

"That's right. I forgot how young she is."

"No, you didn't."

"Well, she's a lovely girl."

"That's enough. Now tell me about you."

"I'm fine. I'm eating, walking and doing my exercises."

"Good."

"Are we done?"

"Are you busy?"

"As a matter of fact, yes."

"What are you up to?"

"Things."

Eddie sighed. "All right, Mom. We love you. Please take care of yourself."

"I love you, too. Come see me sometime."

"We will. Bye now."

He hung up. She sat holding the receiver, hearing the dial tone. The sound of Eddie's voice had affected her more deeply than it should have. He'd called her just two weeks ago, and she'd known right away who it was. Why was this time different? She hadn't been thinking about her husband. That was a lie, one of several she'd just told her son. For some reason, she thought Ed said, "Hi, there" from the great beyond. It was absurd but also frightening. She hoped it never happened again.

Standing at the counter talking to Eddie had tired her legs, and she felt shaky walking back to the table. She sat down heavily and sipped her coffee. It was cold, as was her toast, so she pushed them away and sat, staring out the window.

A few minutes later, she stood up, made sure she felt steady enough, and carried her mug and plate to the sink where she poured the cold coffee down the drain. After tossing the toast in the trash, she walked to the recliner and carefully lowered herself into it. With the remote, she turned the television on. A soap opera was playing. She didn't know which one. They all seemed the same to her. So she turned the television off and closed her eyes.

EIGHT

When she opened her eyes again, it was nearly dark. Between her and the television stood Ed. At first, he looked as solid as any other human being, but then he seemed to dissolve, fading into transparency and finally disappearing. But before he vanished, he said, "It was all a mistake."

At first, she was terrified. Her body went rigid, and she gasped for air. Then she struggled to get out of the chair so she could run. The movement brought agony in her shoulder and only slightly less excruciating pain in the rest of her body. As Ed disappeared, she gave up the fight and fell back, sobbing, overcome with fear and sorrow.

There was more, too. Desperation. She had to know what Ed meant by the mistake. What was the "all" that had gone so wrong. Surely he wasn't talking about their marriage. It had had its ups and downs but, overall, it had worked out well. Besides, why would the other voices be commenting on her marriage? It didn't make any sense.

Of course, none of this made any sense. Not the voices, not the ghost, none of it. She'd been half-asleep. It was just a dream. A nightmare. There was no mistake, just a figment of her imagination brought on by perfectly explainable causes — the wind, the creek.

She'd spent a lot of time when she was younger sitting by Piñon Creek, letting the roar of its descent from its timberline source drown out all other sounds. After a while, the stream took on voices of its own, as if a crowd of the disembodied were carrying on a discussion. She could almost make out individual words but could never quite make sense of the conversation.

What was happening to her now was no different. Except for the apparition. But she could chalk that up to being half-asleep. The difference, though, was that she understood perfectly what the dream voices said, and it was always the same thing.

Gingerly, she scooted forward in the chair, holding her right arm as still as possible, until the footrest lowered, and she could use her left arm to push herself to her feet. The pain was awful, but she knew it wouldn't get any better until she'd taken aspirin and applied the ice pack. She made her way to the kitchen, took three aspirin and assembled the ice pack. Returning to the recliner, she eased herself into it, put the ice pack on her shoulder and waited for the treatment to take effect.

Darkness had come. She decided to leave the lights out and sleep in the recliner again. For what she judged to be about 20 minutes, she forced herself to stay awake. Then she removed the ice pack to avoid overdoing the cold. Years ago, when she'd sprained her ankle playing tennis with Ed, he'd taught her that leaving an ice pack on too long could be harmful. She didn't need any more damage to her shoulder.

The aspirin and cold pack must have helped because when she woke, it was again light outside. Even though she needed to go to the bathroom badly, she had to take her time getting out of the chair. Her joints were stiff from being in one position so long, and the pain was still with her, although not at the same intensity as the night before.

It seemed as if she'd dreamed about playing tennis all night, always with Ed, although he preferred to play with other men. She was beating him, too, floating across the court from shot to shot, answering his best efforts with smooth, graceful forehands and backhands, landing the ball in the exact spot she'd intended.

Ed swore each time he missed a shot, growing angrier and angrier as the game went on. His frustration built to the point where he threw his racquet so it skittered across the court and into the backstop. She just smiled and waited for him to get back into the game. She was having fun, and nothing was going to change that.

She wasn't sure why she experienced such pleasure watching herself defeat her husband in a world that didn't exist, but she did. And there was no harm in it. After all, it was just a dream.

Still, she felt a little guilty. Getting so much enjoyment out of dreaming she beat her husband at tennis seemed petty. The dream didn't mean anything, of course, but still . . . And he'd looked so miserable standing there in front of the television, telling her it was all a mistake. Was he talking about himself? Did he think it was a mistake to be with her?

Ridiculous. That was just a dream, too, something conjured up by pain and too little food. She hadn't eaten at all for about 36 hours. She needed nourishment. After making her way to the bathroom, staggering a bit and using every available piece of furniture and countertop to help her keep her balance, she made her usual breakfast, only this time she added two pieces of toast.

Sitting at the table, her food in front of her, she checked the feeders. The regulars were all present. She decided to try getting back into her routine, using her left hand to write the birds' names in her notebook. Between each addition, she took a bite of toast and a sip of coffee.

Writing with her left hand was slow and awkward, producing a scrawl instead of her usual, slightly twitchy cursive. When she finished listing the morning's birds, she took another bite of toast and sip of coffee.

As she was putting her mug down, the new bird arrived at its favorite place. After a quick look around, it started pecking out seeds and tossing the empty hulls to the ground.

Only the one bird again, maybe male, maybe female. Most of the time, the males were the showy ones, but this could be the showier of the sexes. There was no way to know for sure. But it was spring. A mate might show up any time. If it did, she'd need to have Janet come out and photograph it.

The thought of a possibly more colorful new bird excited her. Even if the difference was more subtle, though, a bird of the opposite sex, as distinctive as this one, would surely indicate a new species. She picked up her binoculars and studied the trees and bushes beyond the feeders. Nothing new. Just a chickadee hanging upside down, feeding on seeds.

She put the binoculars down and stared at the new bird, as if looking at it long enough would reveal its secrets — where it came from, where it went when it left the feeders, whether it was really a new species or maybe a hybrid or a variation from the normal appearance of a known species. She knew there could be a lot of variation within bird species, just as there was among human beings.

The bird flew into the trees along the creek and then crossed it. She followed it with the binoculars as it moved higher, flitting from piñon to juniper to piñon as it made its way uphill. Was it returning to its nesting area or to rejoin its flock? Was it even the same bird she'd seen before? It looked like the same one, but she couldn't be sure.

She hadn't heard it sing because she'd only seen it through the window. Even if she did hear it, she had no way of recording it to give her more evidence. Maybe Janet could help with that, too. She should call later and ask.

The pain in her shoulder had diminished to a dull throb, thanks to the aspirin. Her arm still looked terrible, black and blue tinged with greenish yellow. She seemed to bruise easily these days, the slightest bump leaving a disproportionately large mark. Another gift of aging, she supposed. She would ask about it the next time she visited the doctor, a chore she hated and seldom performed. As she'd once told her husband the physician, "If I go for a checkup, they'll just find something wrong." As long as she could still eat, drink and use the toilet on her own, she saw no reason to ask for trouble.

The old rotary phone jangled again, startling her as it always did. Two calls in two days. She was becoming so popular she'd have to pull the plug to get any peace. She pushed herself up from the table and answered it on the fifth ring instead of the sixth. Progress.

She said, "Hello," her voice raspy because she hadn't used it much for a while.

"Hey, bird lady, you all right?"

She cleared her throat. "Hello, Matt." Matt Enfield had never called her before, so she was immediately suspicious. "I'm fine. Just a frog in my throat. What can I do for you?"

"Janet asked me to call you."

Of course. Janet couldn't stay quiet about the accident. She was a reporter, incapable of keeping anything to herself. Helen wondered if she'd told Matt about the new bird.

"Why would Janet do that?"

"She's worried about you. Thought you might need some help since you hurt your arm."

"There's nothing to worry about."

"Okay. But if you do need anything, call me. Let me give you my cell number."

In spite of her anger, she picked up a pen and a piece of paper and jotted down the number Matt gave her. She'd never use it. There was no need. She'd be fine. She thanked Matt and hung up, anxious to end the conversation in case she might reveal too much.

She hadn't asked Janet to stay quiet about her injury, but she felt betrayed anyway. Now she had to worry that Janet's loose lips might lead to her revealing the new bird. The possibility of that happening made her queasy, so she sat in the recliner to let the nausea subside and the anger pass. If the secret came out, it came out. There was nothing she could do about it.

The phone rang. She struggled to get out of her chair but did it quickly enough to answer on the fourth ring.

"Hello."

"Hi, it's Janet."

She didn't reply.

"Matt tells me you seemed upset when he called. Is everything okay?"

"Why did you tell him about my shoulder?"

"I thought he might be able to help."

"I don't need help."

"Aren't there a lot of things you have to do that take both arms, like using a broom or peeling a potato?"

"I don't eat potatoes."

"You know what I mean. I thought between the two of us, Matt and I could take care of some of the chores until you're better."

"Have you told anyone about the new bird?"

"Not a soul."

"Good. Keep it that way, please."

"I will. Now, do you need anything either Matt or I could help you with?"

"No."

"But you'll let us know if there is."

"I'll think about it."

"That's all we ask."

"All right. Good-bye."

She hung up, replacing the receiver with a little more force than she'd intended. If she needed help, she'd call Janet. She didn't want a strange man coming around, even if Janet seemed to trust him. You never knew about people.

Back in the recliner, she turned on the television. A soap opera was playing again. She didn't care about it, but the actors' voices were somehow comforting. It didn't matter what they said, and she paid no attention to the words, only the rhythm of men's and women's voices rising and falling. As long as she didn't listen to what they were saying, the voices were like a lullaby, calming her. Before long, she fell asleep, letting the voices carry her away.

Then, what had been a gentle sea of sound became a brutal cacophony of screams, each telling her it was all a mistake. She woke gasping, the voices still attacking like clubs, battering her until she cried out, "Stop! Please!" and they abruptly fell silent.

On the television, another soap opera had replaced the one she'd been listening to. A man and a woman were yelling at each other, the woman accusing the man of cheating on her with her sister. She turned the television off and started crying. Then the weeping exploded into loud sobs issuing from depths she didn't know she had, each one bringing another onslaught of pain.

When the sobs subsided and her breathing grew less ragged, she sat still, waiting for the pain to ease. It did lessen, everywhere except her shoulder. After 10 minutes or so, she managed to get out of the recliner and baby-step her way to the kitchen, where she took three aspirin and washed them down with a tumbler of water. She hadn't realized how thirsty she was until she took the first sip and realized the tablets had stuck to her tongue. It took a moment to swallow the aspirin, so she tasted the bitterness and took several large mouthfuls of water to get rid of it.

She decided to skip the ice pack and, after visiting the bathroom, sat down at the table instead, glancing at the clock. It was late afternoon, after 5:00, so the birds were gathering at the feeders for their last meal of the day. She picked up her pen and recorded everything she saw. Nothing unusual, except in the section of the creek she could see through her window.

A gray bird with a plump body and short tail stood on a rock in the middle of the stream, facing away from her. It bobbed up and down as if it had some kind of tic. Then it dove into the water and emerged a few feet upstream with something in its beak and flew a short distance, settling on another rock. It swallowed the food and resumed bobbing.

She hadn't seen an American dipper since the previous autumn, although it was a year-round resident, so she took pleasure in recording it now.

At least one good thing had come from this day.

The crying jag had caught her by surprise again. She hoped it would be the last one. She wasn't sure she could take any more of them. The worst part was not being able to figure out what mistake the voices were talking about and who made it.

Ed had looked so sad, standing there in front of the television. Was he talking about that woman? Was he admitting there was something going on between them? They'd had some awful fights about it. She'd even slapped him, and he'd slapped her back. It might have gotten worse, except 10-year-old Paul wedged himself between them and begged them to stop. They quit hitting each other, but the fight didn't end there. It went on for a couple of days, periods of tense silence punctuated by outbursts of angry recriminations. It became a pattern, and the three kids who still lived at home learned to stay in their rooms, except for meals liberally spiced with invective. In all their married life, it was the worst of times.

Was Ed finally saying he did have an affair? That was ridiculous. She'd come around at last, accepting his word that nothing was going on. But had she, really? Or had she just grown tired of the fight? Her rage had exhausted her. She couldn't eat or sleep. And she only had suspicion on her side. There was no real evidence. Also, she hadn't wanted to have the fight.

As hurt as she was, as betrayed as she felt, she hadn't wanted to fight. At several points in the days-long confrontation, she'd almost given in. She'd almost told Ed she knew she was wrong, apologizing for being so stupid. In the end, that's what she did, and everything returned to normal. Time passed, and she was able to forget the incident happened. Until now.

It had come back like a battering ram, splintering defenses she had built through years of effort. While she'd been hiding behind the castle gate, an army of bitterness had been growing outside. It took one ghost with a sad face and a few vague words about a mistake to destroy that hard-earned bulwark. She wasn't sure which made her angrier, Ed's infidelity or her failure to keep her anguish at bay. There was no point in denying it any longer. She was certain he'd cheated on her at least one time, maybe more.

It was strange, but she felt like the victim of a torture technique called pressing that was popular in England, starting in the 13th Century. She couldn't remember where she'd learned about it, but it had obviously made an impression.

Pressing was designed to compel people who wouldn't enter a plea when they were faced with trial for a crime. If the accused refused to plead guilty or not guilty, they'd be forced to lie on their back while the torturers placed a board on their chest and piled stones on it. The victims had a choice, either enter a plea or be slowly suffocated.

She felt like she'd received a reprieve and all the stones had been removed. Her breathing seemed easier and each breath deeper. It was probably just the aspirin kicking in, but the pain in her shoulder seemed better, too.

She stood and almost toppled from vertigo. Maybe she was reading too much into "the truth will set you free." She sat.

So her revelation hadn't miraculously made her younger, but it had made her feel lighter, freer than she had in a long time. She took off the sling and rested her right arm on the table, slowly straightening it, wincing at the stiffness in her elbow.

What she couldn't understand was why knowing her husband had been unfaithful made her feel the way she did. She should be devastated. The only explanation she could come up with had to do with being devastated for about 40 years and not realizing it. Any pain she felt now was nothing compared to what she'd been hiding all that time.

She wanted to dance but knew it would be asking too much of her body. So she hummed a waltz she'd learned when she was a child and played the table like a piano, an instrument she had an uncomfortable relationship with but worked at mastering until her arthritic fingers became so misshapen she couldn't hit the right keys anymore. On the tabletop, she couldn't make mistakes, and she could imagine herself as a little girl in a pretty white dress, striking the keys with small but straight and flexible fingers.

She hummed and played until her arms grew weary and her voice hoarse. By then, it was dark, but she was far from ready to go to bed. She'd had plenty of sleep. Now she needed to do something constructive. A bath sounded good. It had been four days since her last one, and she figured she must be getting a little ripe.

Using both hands on the tabletop, she pushed up, pleased that the strength seemed to be returning to her right arm and the pressure on her shoulder hadn't hurt too much. The arm was still black, blue, and greenish-yellow, but that would go away. Finally, things were looking up.

She unzipped her pants and let them fall to her ankles, followed by her panties. Then she sat back down to finish the job, pushing her flats off and then unbuttoning her blouse. She couldn't take the garment off the way she usually did. It hurt her shoulder. So she slipped it off her left arm and used that hand to pull it off her right. Only her bra remained, and it proved to be the toughest challenge. She eventually succeeded in removing it after struggling for what seemed like hours, unsnapping it behind her back, using only her left hand.

She wasn't sure why she bothered wearing a bra anyway, except without it her breasts dangled to her waist. It was the curse of being old and well-endowed. Maybe she should try a bra that snapped in front. She'd seen them advertised, but the snap seemed so flimsy, like it could break easily and leave her looking flat-chested and suddenly 20 pounds heavier around the middle. Not a pretty sight. No, she'd stick with the bras that snapped in the back.

Her son Paul had installed a hand bar so she had something to hang onto when she stepped into the bathtub. She used it after she filled the tub with hot water and made sure her soap and shampoo were close at hand. She lay back and let her head sink below the surface of the water for a few seconds. Then, with her left hand, she shampooed her hair and used the soap to cleanse any area that might harbor unpleasant odors.

Getting out of the tub was difficult. She could use her right arm, but the pain shot through her shoulder every time she tried to push herself up so she could step over the rim of the tub. It took what was to her a herculean effort to stand, but she finally accomplished it. Holding the hand bar, she stepped out of the tub and toweled off, wrapping another towel around her head. She kept her hair cut short, so it would only need to be combed out to look just fine.

She left the bathroom and walked, naked, to her dresser, where she pulled out clean panties. She decided to skip the bra. She wasn't going to see anyone, and trying to snap the thing one-handed was way more than she wanted to contend with. She made her way to the hallway leading from her eating and sleeping area to the living room and opened her closet. There wasn't much there, so it took her little time to choose a light, zippered sweater and a pair of elastic-waisted pants. The outfit would be easy to put on and take off, even with only one hand.

Half-sitting on the edge of the bed, she put on her clothes and her red slippers. She felt refreshed, reborn even, as though the water and soap had cleansed more than her body. It would be too much to say she experienced a baptism, but it was certainly a renewal. Tomorrow, she would go back into the world, and she would begin with a croissant and a cup of coffee made from freshly ground beans.

For now, she was content to return to her table and look over her bird list of the day. She ticked off 15 species, including the new bird, and came to American dipper, the last entry.

Where did that come from? She didn't remember seeing a dipper or writing it down. She tried to think back on the day's events, but seeing a dipper wasn't among them. Why would she add a bird she didn't see? Maybe she'd fallen into a reverie, as she sometimes did, and recorded the bird because she wished she'd seen it. At any rate, she couldn't in good conscience leave it on the list, so she scratched it out.

Seeing the dipper on the list left her uneasy. It made no sense. But then, neither did seeing her dead husband and hearing him confess to cheating on her, or at least sort of confess to it. The Ed sighting she could chalk up to a revelatory dream and see it as her subconscious finally waking her up to what she had known all along. The dipper was a different matter. The name was definitely written in her left-handed scrawl, so she'd done it, and no one else had been in the house that day. Then again, she'd been in such a state after the dream, maybe her mind took her someplace she wanted to be instead of leaving her in the dark hole she found herself.

She loved American dippers. They were so odd — little round birds, bobbing up and down in the middle of a rushing stream, dropping into the water and walking on the bottom, against the current, looking for food.

Then it came to her. She'd been like a dipper just then, struggling against the current to find the truth. Maybe that was what caused her to write the bird on her list. Anyway, that was her story and she'd damned well stick to it.

Night had come again, and she needed a good sleep in her bed, not the recliner. She looked at the clock, surprised to see it was 8:15. She took two more aspirin, undressed without too much difficulty, put on her nightgown and got into bed. Some experimentation showed that she could lie on her back and her left side without a great deal of discomfort.

As tired as she was, she couldn't close her eyes. She hated to admit it, but the events of the day, especially Ed's appearance, left her feeling not so much frightened as melancholy. Yes, she was glad to have ferreted out the truth, but she wasn't sure what she could do with it. After the initial feeling of triumph, of having exorcised a demon that had held her captive for so many years, she now felt hollowed out. It was as if something she didn't want but had grown used to were suddenly taken away, and she could feel the empty space it left behind. She had nothing to fill it with, no one to talk to about it, no way to celebrate her victory. No one would ever know what she knew, not Janet, not her children, no one.

She fell asleep and dreamed about the Grand Canyon, where she and Ed had taken their youngest children to show them the magnificent view from the lodge at the north rim. But in the dream, the great natural excavation the Colorado River had carved into the earth seemed bottomless, and she was falling into it with Ed watching from behind the large windows of the lodge viewing room.

She woke screaming, sitting up abruptly as she had the first time she'd heard the voice telling her it was all a mistake. This time, it hurt worse. Her shoulder, wrenched by the sudden movement, felt like it was being torn from her body. She lay back slowly, enduring the arthritic agony because she wasn't sure she could stand it if her shoulder landed too fast and hard. Tears of pain welled. She moaned then sobbed, physical pain and heartbreak conspiring to cause overwhelming misery. For a long time, she lay on her back, letting the tears fall into her pillow.

When she woke again, the sun was up. Although she didn't know what time the nightmare had awakened her, she knew she had slept for hours afterward, uninterrupted, longer than she could remember sleeping at one stretch in decades. Her tears had left her pillow damp, and she realized the bed would be a whole lot damper if she didn't get to the bathroom.

It hurt to get up but not as much as she expected, and she made it to the bathroom without incident. Whatever had come over her after she'd gone to bed seemed much less oppressive now. The hopelessness that had overcome her in the darkness had dissipated. Where she had felt it last night, in the region below her heart, now she had hunger pangs. She was starving. She dressed as quickly as she could, making sure to put on a long-sleeved shirt to hide her bruised right arm, grabbed her car keys and, for the first time in three days, stepped outside.

The birds were busy at the feeders, but she paid them little attention. A croissant and fresh-brewed coffee called to her, and she heeded the summons with single-minded purpose.

Climbing into the Blazer proved easier than she'd thought, and she settled behind the wheel, proud of her ability to adjust to changing circumstances. If she'd had to walk the mile or so to the Double Dyke Bakery she would have done it. She could almost smell the coffee and baked goods as she backed out of the garage and turned down the lane.

She parked in front of the bakery, climbed slowly and carefully out of the Blazer and entered, passing Matt's three-legged mutt Mike lying beside the door, patiently waiting for his master. Inside, she found Janet, Matt, and Sheriff MacGregor at one of the four tables and David and Marge Scott at another. So many people, all greeting her at once, along with Minnie and Tilly who stood behind the counter. Helen said hello to all of them and walked to the counter.

Minnie smiled at her. "Croissant and coffee?"

She nodded. "Yes, please."

Tilly poured a cup of coffee from a pot on a warmer, pulled a croissant from the case, put it on a plate, added a spoonful of strawberry jam and placed it and a knife on the counter as Minnie collected payment.

The coffee smelled delicious, far better, she had to admit, than the freeze-dried stuff she drank at home. Maybe she'd have to get one of those coffee makers after all. Her mouth watered as she carried the croissant and coffee to one of the empty tables. Before she could sit, Janet invited her to join the group at her table. She didn't want to but decided it would be rude not to accept.

Seated at the table with Janet, Matt and Sheriff MacGregor, she couldn't think of anything to say, except, "Nice morning," which brought a nod from the sheriff and "Yes, it is." from Janet and Matt simultaneously.

Matt looked at her right arm. "You doing all right?"

Although it hurt to do it, she picked up her cup with her right hand, took a sip and said, "I'm doing great." Then she tore a piece off her croissant, used the knife to add a little jam and put it in her mouth. It seemed to melt on her tongue, and she closed her eyes, smiling.

When she opened her eyes, the sheriff was smiling, too. "I don't think I've ever seen anyone appreciate a croissant quite that much."

Embarrassed, she swallowed quickly and took another sip of coffee. It was the first time Sheriff MacGregor had spoken to her in months, and his jovial tone raised her suspicions. She wondered if Janet or Matt had said something to him about her fall. She glanced at them to spot any tell-tale signs that they'd given away her secret. They both smiled at her with that gentle kindness that young adults reserve for children and old people. It infuriated her, but she smiled back. "They're the best I've ever had," she said.

From behind the counter, Minnie laughed. "Thank you. Just for that . . ."

Tilly finished Minnie's sentence. ". . . the next one's free." Minnie pulled another croissant from the display case and brought it to the table.

Staring at the puffy pastry in front of her, Helen sighed. "I can't possibly eat that."

Minnie put her hands on her hips. "Of course you can, you're . . ."

". . . so skinny you disappear if you turn sideways," Tilly said.

"I suppose I could share it."

Minnie stomped her foot. "Don't you dare. Take it home and have it later, but . . ."

" . . . don't wait too long, or it'll dry out." Minnie nodded assent as Tilly finished her thought for her. Minnie brought a paper bag, slipped the croissant into it and left it on the table.

The partly eaten pastry still beckoned, so she tore off another piece, smeared some jam on it and put it in her mouth. This time, she kept her eyes open, trying to savor the buttery sweetness without making a show of it.

Matt ended the pause in the conversation. "How are the birds?"

Had Janet told Matt about the new bird? That would be a worse betrayal than talking about her fall. She glanced at Janet but couldn't detect any sign of guilt. Still, she wasn't satisfied.

"Why do you ask?"

Matt seemed a little surprised by the question. "Just curious. Seen anything unusual?"

Now she was sure Janet had given her away. She gave the traitor a scathing look, to which Janet reacted with what looked like real shock.

Sheriff MacGregor apparently saw the silent interchange. "What's wrong? Are you okay?"

Realizing her reaction must have seemed both unwarranted and extreme, she forced a smile. "I'm fine." She sipped her coffee and prepared another bite of croissant.

Matt seemed concerned. Janet had probably not told him that the new bird was a secret, so she gave him what she thought was her nicest smile. "I thought I saw something new, but it turned out to be just a white-crowned sparrow getting its spring plumage.”

She again glanced at Janet, whose look of surprise gave her some satisfaction. Matt kept his eyes on her, not giving away his collusion with Janet. Helen ate the last of the croissant and took a final swallow of coffee.

“I have to go now. Have some shopping to do.” She stood, picked up her bagged croissant and headed for the door. Matt and Sheriff MacGregor stood. Janet remained seated, the surprise still on her face. With a wave to Minnie and Tilly, who smiled and waved back, she walked out to the Blazer, relieved to be out from under scrutiny.

Before climbing in behind the steering wheel, she took a deep breath. Her shoulder hurt. She needed some aspirin, but she could buy some at the Valley View Market. After the last few days, she was getting low on the tablets anyway. She drove the block to the store.

She’d taken a bottle of aspirin from among the few health-care items the market offered and swallowed two tablets when Janet entered. Janet had to know she was in the store. The Blazer sat in plain view outside.

Removing her sunglasses, Janet looked around the store, searching until she found Helen. The temptation to pretend she didn’t notice Janet took over for a second, but Helen knew it wouldn’t do any good, so she chose confrontation instead.

Striding across the room, Janet stopped in front of her. “What was that all about?”

“What do you mean?”

“You know what I mean. As soon as Matt asked if you’d seen any new birds, you went all evil eye on me.”

“If you know it was about the bird, why not just say so.”

“Okay. I didn’t tell Matt about your new bird. It hurts that you’d believe I would.”

“You told him about my shoulder.”

“I never said I wouldn’t.”

“You didn’t?”

“No, I didn’t.”

“Well, you should have.”

“You’re changing the subject. I promised I wouldn’t say anything to anyone about the bird, and I didn’t.”

“All right. I’m sorry.”

Janet smiled. “Apology accepted. But you need to know who your friends are and give them the benefit of the doubt.”

“Okay.” She gave Janet a little smile. “I need to get going.”

“Got a pressing appointment?”

“Need to do some cleaning. Excuse me.” She walked around Janet and out the door.

The market’s proprietor, Joe Jackson, followed her. “Forget something?”

She turned toward him. "What?"

"You didn't pay."

Embarrassed, she followed him back inside. Janet stood at the checkout counter, her few purchases in front of her. She was grinning. "Don't you hate it when a grand exit goes wrong?"

"Be quiet."

"I wouldn't have taken you for a shoplifter. Rough childhood? Bad company? Kleptomania? How about an interview? You can tell me all about your criminal past."

"That's enough." Helen paid for her aspirin and left.

On the way home, she stopped at the post office and had no trouble remembering her box number. When she pulled into her garage, she felt exhausted and ashamed. She'd misjudged Janet and walked out of the Valley View Market without paying. What else could go wrong?

Soon after she entered her house, the phone rang. She'd been heating the water for coffee and getting ready to eat the croissant she'd been given for her rave review at the bakery. She picked up the phone.

"Hello?"

It was Janet. "You got an email from Beekman."

"Already?"

"It isn't the Pony Express, you know."

"But why so soon?"

"Why not?"

"If he thought it might be something new, he would have done some research. That takes time."

"So bad news?"

"Don't know. What does the email say?"

"I thought you should read it first. I'll print it out and bring it to you."

"No, no, I'll come to you. Be there in a few minutes."

She hung up, turned off the burner under the tea kettle and put the croissant back in its paper bag. She'd try to get to it later, even though it surely wouldn't be at its best.

When Helen arrived at the newspaper office, Janet stood at the door. She climbed out of the Blazer as quickly as she could and entered the office. Janet handed her the piece of paper with Beekman's response.

"Greetings," it began. "I have reviewed your description. You should know that the last new bird species identified in the United States, the Bryan's shearwater, was discovered 10 years ago in a museum. Before then, the most recent finding occurred about 47 years ago. Living specimens of the shearwater have yet to be found.

"I suspect your bird might be a hybrid, specifically a cross between a golden-crowned and white-crowned sparrow (*Zonotrichia atricapilla* and *Zonotrichia leucophrys*). Both occur in your area, although the golden-crowned is a rarity. The particular hybrid I'm referring to was found in Alaska in 2009.

"Thank you for your inquiry."

The note was signed, "Robert Beekman, Ph.D."

She handed the paper to Janet who scanned it and said, "What a prick."

Helen shook her head. "It's as if he never knew me. Can you look up the hybrid he's talking about for me?"

Janet sat at her computer and searched for the hybrid.

"Odd that the new species the prick mentioned is called the Bryan's shearwater. Maybe it's a good sign, a precedent. You can call your new one the Bryan's whatever."

"Naming species you discover after yourself is bad form."

"Why?"

"It's arrogant. If you're going to name it after a person, make it somebody like a family member or someone you respect."

Janet took her hands off the keyboard and clapped. "Found it."

On the screen was a bird that looked little like the one she'd described. Other than the yellow median crown stripe and black lateral crown stripes, there were only general similarities. The hybrid did have yellow superciliums, but its lores were gray. The eyelines were black instead of brown. The mandibles were pale instead of black and the throat and malars gray instead of white. As for the breast, sides, flanks and belly, all were gray or brownish gray, not white. Overall, the rest of the bird was brownish gray, the tail showing none of the reddish hue. The undertail coverts were also brownish gray instead of white.

How Beekman could have dismissed her bird as a golden-crowned and white-crowned sparrow hybrid mystified and angered her. She grabbed the email printout from the table where Janet had left it, wadded it up in a tight ball and threw it at a nearby wastebasket, missing it. The paper wad rolled a few feet and disappeared under a chair.

She started to walk to the chair. "Sorry, I'll get that."

Janet grasped her left wrist. "Don't worry about it. You'll just find a bunch of other junk under there, and I'd rather you didn't."

She took the seat next to Janet's desk, an image of Beekman from 30 years earlier forming in her mind. She remembered the contempt he'd shown her, the attempt to dismiss her identification of the king rail she'd heard but not yet seen. All the hurt came flooding back, and then the tears came. As hard as she fought them, they came. Janet's face dissolved into a blur. Then the blur came toward her as Janet leaned in and took her left hand in both of hers. At first, she tried to pull away but realized the touch brought a little comfort. She let Janet hold her hand.

"The guy's a jerk. His bird is bogus. Nothing like yours. We'll try another way."

Helen's tears streaked her cheeks, but they'd stopped flowing. "He's the only ornithologist I know, and he's very good. I don't know where else to turn."

Janet let go of her hand and turned back to the computer. "That's what the internet is for, my dear. Let's go hunting."

She brought up Google, typed in "leading ornithologists united states" and leaned back in her chair. The results appeared immediately, and she scanned the first few pages.

"Mostly associations and such. I think we need to try a different approach. Any thoughts?"

"How about starting with 'leading university ornithology programs United States?'"

"Say, you're getting pretty good at this. We can find the names by finding the programs."

She typed the search phrase in. The first result was what looked like a guide to all the universities offering graduate studies in ornithology.

"Too broad." Janet scrolled down to an entry about the best university for ornithology. It offered another, very short, list.

"Looks like Cornell University in Ithaca, New York, is the best, not only in the U.S. but in the world." Janet turned to her and smiled. "Want to start there?"

"Let's do it."

"Let me just check my email before we dive into this." She brought up a screen full of messages to be opened and scanned it. "Uh, oh."

"Is something wrong?"

"It seems your professor has more to say." She clicked on the subject line, and the full message appeared on the screen. There was no greeting this time.

"After further consideration, I've decided to look into your bird a little further. I'd like to visit the area of the sighting and see what more I can learn. This should happen soon, as I can't be sure how long the bird will remain in the vicinity.

"You've provided information about the environment but nothing about the specific location. Please let me know exactly where to go."

Helen snorted, a habit she'd picked up from her father and had been trying to get rid of her whole life. "I'd love to."

"Now, now. At least he has the brains to reconsider."

"You're right. Let's tell him where I am."

Janet hit Reply and typed in "Valley View, CO. Ask for directions to my home at the newspaper office."

"That work?"

"Sure. This way you can warn me when he arrives, and I can have the shotgun ready."

"Shotgun? You own a shotgun?"

"Of course not. But I was a crack shot when I was in college."

"Really?"

"You'd be surprised."

"I am surprised."

"There's more."

"Tell me."

"Another time. Right now, I need to get home." She didn't, of course, but she felt tired and didn't want to work at keeping up her end of the conversation. All she wanted was time to finish her croissant. Also, her shoulder hurt. She needed some aspirin and an ice pack.

The croissant had dried out by the time she got back to it. She popped it in the microwave and returned it to a semblance of freshness. With strawberry jam, it tasted just fine. She'd already taken the aspirin, and the ice pack waited in the freezer.

As she ate, she speculated about Robert Beekman. When he was her professor, he was at least 25 years younger than she was, so that would make him around 60 years old. He should be retiring before too long.

She wondered what made him so angry. He hadn't always been like that. When she first met him, on the day she started taking his class, he had seemed outgoing and friendly. As the semester went on and her wetland project stretched into a second semester, he seemed impressed with her ability to identify the preserved skins, as he called them, of birds from around the world. He commented on her skill at determining the features that differentiated one species from another, even when others found it difficult to see the variations in plumage, bill shape and other identifying marks.

On one occasion, he told her he was getting close to finishing a major project, a study that would change ornithology forever. But when she asked for details, he closed down, saying, "No, I can't take the chance that word will get out before I'm ready. What I've discovered will make history, not only in ornithology but in all of biology."

A few months later, the betrayal came, and she never heard anything more about the revolutionary discovery. She decided the study must have failed to back up Beekman's hypothesis and been shelved. After she graduated, she tried to find something about Beekman's work but couldn't locate anything except some technical papers about the differences between eastern and western meadowlarks and the effects of certain pesticides on pintails, among other topics. She found the information interesting but hardly earthshaking.

Now she confronted the prospect of seeing Beekman face-to-face again. She felt scared and angry — and ashamed that the fucking asshole could make her feel either. The power he had over her had no basis in real life. It emerged from nothing and got her nowhere. Maybe she could find a way to get rid of it when he arrived on her turf.

Of course, he could conclude that the new bird wasn't really new at all.

Then she'd be helpless, without hope because she held only a Bachelor of Science degree, not a Ph.D. That's what happens when you depend on fucking assholes for confirmation.

She knew she couldn't let her leftover rage show when Beekman arrived. She'd have to be nice and respectful if she wanted him to work with her, and she desperately wanted to be part of the process. She'd have to play pupil to his master, as much as it galled her.

As she bit off another piece of her croissant, the new bird appeared again, still alone. She wondered why. It was spring, time to mate and nest. Was this a male or a female? Either way, there should be another one. Maybe there was. In some bird species, the males and females look alike. It doesn't occur often, but it happens. Still, no two birds of the same species are exactly alike. Individuals differ from each other in what, to human eyes, are often nearly indiscernible ways. So far, though, she'd seen none of those oh-so-subtle differences. This appeared to be the same bird over and over. And, if it had a mate, the two of them should be together some of the time. Can't mate if you don't date or at least meet up once in a while.

Beekman. She hadn't thought about his name until just now. She wondered if it was one of the reasons he'd become an ornithologist. But if that were the case, he'd be opening himself to jokes and, as far as she knew, he'd shown no signs of having a sense of humor, especially about himself. Surely, when he started studying ornithology, other students would have pointed out the problem. If he weren't such a fucking asshole, she would have been tempted to feel sorry for him.

The phone rang. She removed the ice pack from her shoulder and got up to answer it. As always, she was a little wobbly and used the chair to steady herself.

It was Janet calling again. "He'll be here in two days."

"Who?"

"Beekman. Are you okay?"

That was strange. She'd been thinking of little else but Beekman since she'd arrived at home. "Of course, I'm okay. You just caught me off-guard. So he'll be here Saturday."

"Yep, he figures around three."

"Looking forward to it."

"No, you're not."

"No, I'm not. But I do want to get this thing settled."

She said goodbye, retrieved the ice pack from the freezer and sat down at the table. Before applying the ice, she put a liberal dollop of jam on the last bite of her croissant and ate it. Somehow, it seemed to calm her, allow her to push Beekman to the back of her mind and focus on the pleasure it brought her.

NINE

When Beekman arrived in Valley View, Janet let Helen know he was on his way to her house. She met him, standing on the front porch. He looked a little nervous as he got out of his car and held up his right hand in greeting. She raised her right hand as high as she could in response. He didn't smile, and neither did she.

Beekman opened the rear door and pulled out a pair of binoculars, which he hung around his neck, and a camera bag. "Is it here now?"

"It was a few minutes ago."

"Show me."

She stepped aside as he climbed the porch stairs and walked past her into the house, where he waited inside the door. She followed him in and led him down the hallway. When they arrived at the windows looking out on the feeders, the new bird wasn't there. Beekman took his jacket off, sat down in her chair and pushed her notebook aside as if it were in the way. She took a seat to his left.

He used his binoculars, an expensive-looking pair of Swarovskis, to scan the trees and bushes around the feeders then lowered them to his chest.

"You've only seen the one?"

"That's right."

"You sure?"

"As sure as I can be."

She studied his face, trying not to be obvious about it. He looked all of 70, with deep creases around his mouth and his eyes heavily hooded. His hair had turned entirely gray, but it wasn't yet white, like hers. It had thinned considerably, too, showing a fair-sized bald spot on top. He'd put on some weight, his belly hanging over his belt like bread dough over the edge of a baking pan. Hardly an intimidating figure.

Yet intimidated she was and afraid if she challenged his arrogance he would simply go away and leave her without support. So she sat, having given up her place so Beekman could get the best view and allowing him to push aside the records she'd kept faithfully all these years. Her embarrassment returned, along with her anger. She couldn't help it.

"So what made you change your mind?"

He looked away from the feeders at her. "What do you mean?"

"You came to take a look after all."

"Oh. Yes, I decided I'd been a little hasty. I still think it's a hybrid, but I want to be sure."

The new bird flew from the river birch to the thistle-seed feeder, the movement catching Beekman's eye. He raised the binoculars and focused them.

"Interesting." He said it without much inflection, as though he were a bit bored by it all. "It's almost certainly an *emberizidae.*"

He lowered the glasses and looked at her. "A sparrow, longspur, bunting, junco or towhee."

She could feel the blood rise in her face. "Yes, I know."

He ignored her, turning back to the bird. "I'd opt for sparrow — specifically, genus *zonotrichia,* which includes the white-crowned, golden-crowned and white-throated, and which helps support my hybrid hypothesis. The yellow lores and yellow median crown stripe suggest a cross between a golden-crowned and a white-throated rather than a golden-crowned and white-crowned."

He smiled a small, tight smile. "I'm surprised you didn't see it."

Again, she felt the heat in her face. "I've never seen a white-throated sparrow on a feeder, and I believe golden-crowned sparrows are also ground feeders."

His smile turned a bit tighter. "Although the crown stripe and lores are not definitive, they are strong evidence of cross-breeding. I'll need . . ."

The phone interrupted him. She stood to answer it and had to lay a hand on the table to steady herself. She could see Beekman's eyes widen, and she immediately took her hand away from the table, strode to the phone and answered it.

"Hi, it's Janet. Is Beekman still there?"

"Yes."

"Somebody sent him an email to my address. It looks important."

"How do you know?"

"The subject line uses the word 'critical.'"

"I'll tell him." She hung up and turned to Beekman.

Janet says you have an email. Something "critical.'"

Beekman stood and put his jacket on. "Thanks. I couldn't take a chance on a bad internet connection out here, so I gave my assistant that address in case anything came up that couldn't wait until I get back."

"You don't need to explain. Janet doesn't mind."

"She wouldn't open it, would she?"

"No, Janet may be a reporter, but she only sticks her nose where it doesn't belong when she smells a story."

"And a mysterious visit from an ornithologist of some renown doesn't smell like a story?"

"She knows why you're here. I asked her to keep it to herself, at least for now."

"That's a good call. I'd hate to see her waste her time on nothing. I'm sure she has a lot of real news to report."

He walked into the hallway, and she followed him to the front door and out onto the porch, where he paused before descending the stairs.

"I'll be back tomorrow morning, early."

"All right."

He left the porch and drove away without another word. She walked back to her table and reclaimed her chair, moving the notebook back in front of her.

Why had she said anything about the new bird to that arrogant jerk? He had clearly decided what it was and was just stringing her along for the fun of it. Why did he hate her so much? She hadn't done anything to him. He'd taken something she loved, studying birds, and turned it against her, treating her as if she were both ignorant and stupid. The knot in her stomach clenched until it hurt, causing her to double over until her head lay on the table. Then, as much as she hated it, the tears came, just as they had on that day at the wetland when he'd told her what he thought of her.

Eventually, the tears stopped, and she raised her head from the table. To her surprise, the knot in her gut had relaxed, and she felt hungry. Of course, it had been hours since she'd eaten. She hobbled to the kitchen, her legs stiff from sitting so long. Dusk had arrived, so she turned on the light over the sink before opening the refrigerator. There wasn't much there. She reached for the bread, butter and strawberry jam. Some things you could rely on.

Later, after finishing her meal, she turned off the light and stepped outside onto the back deck where, even in the darkness, she could see the creek, it's rapids flashing white as the water that had started from a placid, half-frozen lake fed by snowmelt crashed toward its burial under the San Luis Valley sand. It was such a beautiful stream, lined with deep green moss, river birches, narrow-leafed cottonwoods and other moisture-loving plants. It had a rich smell that it shared with all the streams in this part of the country — an earthy, sweet odor that arose from decay, emerging life and the on-going tasks of living and dying.

She breathed deeply and looked up. The stars on this clear night had a three-dimensional look. They shone in layer upon layer, the farthest ones forming a river of dim light. She could almost believe, if she stood tall enough, stretched her body to its limit, her head would be among the stars, and they would float around her like fiery bubbles.

She closed her eyes, imagining what it would be like to be connected to stars and earth, to smell the world of the creek, to hear its violent fall and yet to see and feel the light and heat of those distant balls of fire as they floated around her, close enough to touch.

But this was silly, losing herself in ridiculous fantasies. It wasn't like her at all. Life had taught her to be hard-headed about some things, and she had little patience for the woo-woo meanderings of the new agers who had started invading Valley View a few years ago and seemed to grow more numerous by the month.

She'd spoken to one of them just a year ago or so, an effort to both understand them and learn what they were up to. It was a short conversation.

"Why are you here?" she had asked the thin young woman with long, stringy blond hair, holey blue jeans and a T-shirt that showed her braless nipples. A quartz crystal hung from a chain around her neck.

"What do you mean?"

"Exactly what I said. Why are you here?"

"Do you mean here on Earth, or here in Valley View?"

"Let's start with here in Valley View."

"My spirit brought me to this place."

"So you have a personal spirit?"

"It's my own, yes."

"Does it talk to you?"

"Oh, yes, all the time."

"Has it ever told you you're bonkers?"

The young woman frowned. "You are not a nice person. I think I'll go now."

"Goodbye, and say hi to your spirit for me."

Thinking about the confrontation later, she decided she might have been a little hard on the woo-woo crystal gazer and maybe misunderstood what she was saying about her personal spirit. Still, she doubted it would have made any difference to her opinion.

She'd watched as the newcomers came and went, some of them staying for just a few weeks, others remaining for years. They set up shop, selling crystals, of course, doing Tarot readings and trying to sell their "art." They lived in lean-tos and tents. Some of them built houses out of hay bales. She researched the bale house phenomenon and discovered it made sense. It was cheap, and the hay provided good insulation, a plus in Valley View winters.

But there was something haphazard about their way of life. It seemed unorganized and without real aim or purpose except their own gratification. Yet they seemed to look down on the locals. It was hard to accept an air of superiority from people who smelled like cabbage cooking and looked like they hadn't eaten for a month.

She asked Sheriff McGregor if the invaders were breaking any laws, but he said they weren't. The land they'd settled on was private property, and the woman who owned it had given them permission to use it. As long as they didn't violate any land-use regulations, which were pretty lax in Saguache County, they were free to stay as long as they liked.

So she'd learned to live with the riffraff. Of course, she didn't buy any crystals, subject herself to any readings or purchase any of the works that passed for art. The Double Dyke Bakery, Valley View Market, post office and library provided everything she needed.

She went back in the house, flipping on the light over the table as she entered and taking a seat. Her notebook lay in front of her, and she opened it to enter the birds she'd seen during the day. That done, she went to bed, but found it hard to sleep because she knew Beekman would be back in the morning. She wanted nothing more than for him to go away and never come back. But she knew what she wanted wasn't what she needed.

After most of a night spent awake rather than asleep, she finally drifted off, only to be shocked back to consciousness by the crack of a gun firing. Ignoring the pain, she got out of bed as quickly as she could, threw on her robe and made her way to the front door.

She found Beekman between the house and the garage, facing the feeders and holding a shotgun, its barrel pointed toward the ground. He saw her standing on the porch and waved. Her knees started to buckle, and she grabbed the porch railing for support.

"What have you done?"

He didn't answer. Instead, he walked toward the feeders. She watched him as he approached the thistle seed tube, now shattered, and bent down to pick something off the ground. He brought it to her. The new bird lay in his hand, flecks of blood spotting its feathers. He smiled.

"Collecting a specimen. I already got some good photos. I'll send a check to cover the cost of the feeder."

She could have shot him with his own gun. "But why?"

"You know why. We need it to determine whether it's a hybrid or a new species. The DNA will tell us."

"You had no right to do this."

"Actually, I had every right. My collector's permit says I do."

"But you shot it on my property."

"I have your permission to be here, and you invited me to help you identify this bird. I'm using the best means possible to do that."

The entire time, she'd been staring at the dead bird in Beekman's hand. Now she looked up and away down her lane. She saw his car parked about 100 feet away.

"You didn't want me to hear you." She probably wouldn't have anyway, but Beekman didn't know about her hearing problem. "You didn't want me to know you were here until you'd killed the bird."

He didn't say anything, just stood there with that little smile on his face. Then he reached into his jacket pocket, produced a plastic sandwich bag, dropped the dead bird into it and walked away. She followed him to his car where he opened the rear door and dropped the bird into an ice chest on the seat.

He closed the door, opened the front driver's side door and got in. After closing that door, he started the car, opened the window and looked at her as if he had something to say. She stepped closer.

"If I have a chance, I'll let you know what I find."

She wanted to scream at him, to tell him just how vile she thought he was, but all she could get out was, "You fucking asshole."

At first, he seemed shocked, but then he laughed. He was still laughing as he drove toward the house, used the circle drive to turn around and passed her on the way out to the main road.

When Beekman's car had disappeared, she set the tears and the wracking sobs free because not allowing them to escape might well have killed her. The pressure of the rage filling her head and chest would have been too much for her body to withstand. In her entire life, she had never felt such hatred for another human being. Combined with her grief over the death of a creature that had become so important to her, her hatred created a force that, left to its own devices, might, in her mind, devastate the earth for miles a-round, even as it utterly destroyed her.

The outburst lasted for a long time. When it finally abated, she felt exhausted, almost too weak to walk. Somehow, she managed to make it to the thistle-seed feeder where the new bird had perched before Beekman shot it. She took it down and dropped it on the ground beside the garage. She couldn't stand to look at it anymore.

She entered the house through the back door and sat at the table, staring at the emptiness that, a short time ago, was the new bird's favorite feeder. When she closed her eyes, she saw the bird lying in Beekman's hand, its life over in a second. She hadn't felt such loss and grief since Ed died. It was ridiculous, of course. This was a bird, after all, not a human being. But the sadness she felt contained such an abundance of rage that it could not be dismissed as sentimentality. The bird wasn't a pet whose death caused pain that would eventually ease. In a little more than a week, it had become central to her life, a source of excitement and purpose she hadn't felt since the year she'd studied the wetland.

During those twelve months, she had spent so much time observing the birds that she had neglected her responsibilities as a wife and mother. She hadn't cared. Her study occupied all her attention. The long summer days kept her out late, so she let Ed and the boys who were still at home fend for themselves. Ed took to eating out, and the boys ate cereal or sandwiches they made themselves. She hired a cleaning woman to keep the place presentable.

Even though the study took up most of every day and limited her ability to do much of anything else, she felt freer than she had in years. When it was over and she'd written it up, she was at a loss. The idea of going back to the way things had been before frightened her. She had trouble sleeping, and constant nausea kept her from eating.

Ed and the boys didn't seem to notice, even when she lost 30 pounds and grew more and more listless. They expected her to pick up where she'd left off when she started the study, and she had no reason not to. She was finished with her degree, and the thought of studying for a master's with Robert Beekman was too awful to contemplate. She would just have to put on her big girl face and start behaving like an adult.

Forcing herself back into the routine she'd followed before the study tested her will more than anything she'd ever done. When she had a moment to herself, she cried. Every day seemed like a long walk along a tightrope, with the temptation to let herself fall off into a boiling cauldron of all-consuming rage a constant companion. She knew the anger showed in the way she spoke to Ed and the boys, and she tried to control it. Mostly, she was fairly successful. For the most part, the family seemed oblivious, and that's the way she told herself she wanted it.

As the weeks and months passed, the anger became sadness, which was easier to hide. She still had little appetite, but she could eat ice cream without waking the nausea. She gained about 20 pounds. Before long, she settled back into the role of doctor's wife and, except for the persistent sense of sadness, felt pretty much the way she had before her time in the field.

But the new bird was different. No longer did she have to answer to a husband and kids or the duties inherent in her role as doctor's wife. Her anger lived unbounded in both its intensity and its extent. She could allow it to thrive without worrying about how it would affect those close to her.

That wasn't all, though. This anger far outweighed any sadness she felt about the new bird's death. She'd chosen sadness the last time. Now rage ruled, and she intended to let it reign unfettered. She was done weeping. It was time for dry-eyed, clear-eyed action. And it was up to her and her alone to make things right.

TEN

When she'd first tried to follow the new bird as it left the feeder, she'd seen it fly generally uphill toward the higher elevations. It made sense. Beyond her back fence, the national forest had been designated a wilderness area a number of years ago, so it was relatively unspoiled.

Valley View and the mountains rising above it attracted a few visitors but could hardly be called a tourist mecca. The birdlife in this part of the Sangre de Cristos hadn't been studied extensively, so it was possible that a yet-unknown species had existed here without drawing notice. It would be even likelier if the population were small and non-migratory. If the birds migrated, they'd more likely be seen.

All she had to do was find at least one more new bird in several hundred square miles of mountainous terrain. She'd need a few things, starting with a camera. It was time for another visit to the library.

She stopped at the *Valley View Mountaineer* office to talk to Janet and give herself a cover story. When she walked in, Janet was working at her computer. She looked up quickly and returned her attention to the screen.

"How'd it go with Professor Stuffed Shirt."

"He's gone."

Janet stopped typing and turned in her chair. "Gone? Why?"

"He wouldn't say. I guess he got what he came for."

"So nothing about your bird being a new species."

"Nope."

"What a dick."

"I prefer fucking asshole."

"That works, too."

"Anyway, I'm glad he's gone."

"Want to try another ornithologist?"

"I think I'll give Beekman a chance to review what he has and get back to me. Maybe then I'll tell him I think the flock — if it exists — is somewhere up toward the lake. Or maybe not."

"Why do you think the flock is up there?"

"Just a hunch."

"How long you willing to wait?"

"I'll give him a month or so."

"That long?"

"It takes time to do the research."

"Okay, but what'll you do in the meantime?"

"Observe and record."

"Sounds very scientific — or maybe more like espionage."

"It'll keep me busy."

Janet asked her how her arm was doing and made a little more small talk, then asked, "Plan on another croissant soon?"

She hesitated. "Sure. Maybe Friday. Then I think I'll spend a couple weeks visiting the boys."

"A road trip? I thought you hated leaving Valley View."

"Guess I'm feeling adventurous. Besides, I'd like to see how they're getting along in their own habitat."

"That's a lot of driving. I assume you're not flying."

"Never again. I hate it."

"Okay, then. See you Friday?"

"Yep. Wouldn't miss that croissant."

She left the newspaper office and drove to the library, where, as always, she ignored the single computer available for patrons and picked up some outdoor magazines from the periodicals section. She scanned the advertisements. When she found a product that interested her, she wrote it down, along with the name of the company selling it and the phone number. By the time she was finished, she had a list of 25 items.

As soon as she got home, she started calling the numbers she'd written down and ordering the products. They included a digital camera and a 200-600mm lens, which set her back almost $3,500, but she decided it was worth it if she could get good photos.

She hadn't hiked in the mountains since Ed died, limiting her walking to forays into the woods around her house. In her mind, she was still young and strong, but she knew her body wouldn't agree. When just standing up posed the risk of a bad fall, climbing a mountain seemed at least foolhardy and, at most, insane. But she was willing, even eager to take the chance that somebody would find her corpse rotting away among the aspen leaves and limber pine needles. She could think of far worse ways to go.

Also on her list was camping gear, chosen for its light weight — backpack, sleeping bag and pad, one-person tent, flashlight, solo cook set, rain poncho, many packages of freeze-dried food and other items she thought she might find useful. She'd take one change of clothing and a new pair of boots that would protect her ankles and, she hoped, help prevent slips and falls. If she ate only twice a day, she figured she could stay out for ten days. Should she fail to find another new bird in that time, at least she'd know she'd tried.

All her gear would arrive within the week. That gave her time to have one last croissant before she disappeared into the wilderness. The fact that no one would know where she was scared and excited her. She had butterflies, something she hadn't felt since she was a little girl about to perform at a piano recital. She hoped this adventure would turn out better than that one.

But that wasn't quite true. She'd experienced the butterflies more recently, though still quite a while ago. They came before the first time she and Ed slept together. Once they were in bed, the sensation disappeared almost immediately, replaced by a passion they shared until he left to join the Navy without saying a word to her until the deed was done. He volunteered, even though the Vietnam War doctor draft would have probably gotten him anyway.

She could understand his sense of duty, but she suspected his sense of adventure had more to do with his decision to sign up without the excuse of a draft. He also knew she would try to talk him out of it because their first child was on the way. He enlisted secretly to avoid any discussion. Eddie was born while Ed was training to be a flight surgeon and she was living with her parents.

She'd never told him how angry she was with him for abandoning her. It didn't seem right to attack him for serving the country, so she kept it to herself. But some of the passion she'd felt when they'd first married had gone. They still had sex pretty frequently. After all, they'd had four more babies. It was different, though, more mechanical, less spontaneous, as if she were holding back, unwilling to invest herself completely in the act. For his part, Ed didn't seem to notice any difference, but he never talked about his time in the service. Now that she thought about it, she hadn't asked. It was like a secret they kept from each other, a fuse they didn't dare light.

Ed wrote to her sporadically while he was gone, revealing nothing about where he was and little about what he was doing. Mostly, he asked about Eddie and her parents. With one letter, he included a photo of himself in a white jacket, pants and shoes, his black hair combed back, holding a cigarette and smiling in a cocky way that accentuated his good looks. It was the only thing, besides the few letters, she had to mark passage of the year he was away.

She put thoughts of Ed aside and focused on her search for another bird like the one she'd lost to Beekman and his shotgun. She decided that, once she'd reached a point about halfway to timberline, she'd move off the trail and find a campsite away from any prying eyes. Then she'd take off in a different direction each day until she'd explored as much territory as she could. She knew the chances of finding anything within the restricted area she'd be able to cover were remote, but she had only untrustworthy legs to do the job. She'd have to make the most of her limited abilities and hope for the best.

The new bird had flown toward the canyon where the trail to Darkling Lake started. It was good habitat for birds and animals, with lots of cover and abundant water. If she were a bird and she wanted to expand her horizons, she'd choose a route that provided water and cover. It made sense, and it was the only plan she could come up with.

At least her shoulder felt much better. She no longer needed the aspirin or cold pack and, as long as she didn't try to roll over on her right side, it didn't interfere with her sleep. Full range of motion hadn't returned yet, but the shoulder felt a little less stiff every day. Before long, it would be back to normal, with only the arthritis left to contend with.

The hike to Darkling Lake began at 8,610 feet above sea level. The lake was at 11 ,840 feet, a distance of well under a vertical mile. From the trailhead to the lake, the path was more than five and a half miles long. Its steepness and many switchbacks made the trek seem even longer. She intended to climb only halfway to the lake before making camp, but she had no illusions about the effort it would take to cover two and a half miles on that trail, especially carrying a backpack, no matter how light she managed to keep it. And that five miles didn't include the three she needed to cover to get to the trailhead. She would have to camp at least once before she got to the starting point.

When she finished ordering her equipment and supplies, she sat down at the table and watched the mountain chickadees at the feeders and the dark-eyed juncos on the ground cleaning up. She should replace the thistle-seed feeder. She could order a new one by phone now, but that felt like a betrayal of the new bird. The empty place in the feeder array stood for a loss she felt as deeply as any she'd experienced in her life.

The connection she'd developed with that bird was all in her head, of course. She knew that. The bird could have no such feelings for her. It was an animal, operating on instinct, taking advantage of a plentiful supply of food but without gratitude or any recognition of her generosity or caring. It was not a member of her family or a friend. It wasn't human. To ascribe human emotion and behavior to a bird was absurd, a device for children's books and Disney movies.

What was it called when somebody gave animals human feelings and human traits? Anthropomorphism. The pathetic fallacy. She was a little proud of herself for remembering those terms from classes she'd taken so many years ago.

She couldn't afford to think of birds as having human characteristics. Flights of fancy like that destroyed objectivity, hampered vision with a distorting film of emotion. If she could do away with emotions altogether, she would be happy. But happiness was an emotional state, a contentment that hadn't been part of her life for a long time, if ever.

She'd just have to keep her emotions at bay as much as possible, even though, when she thought about the bird lying dead in Beekman's hand, she wanted to take his gun and shoot him. At close range, birdshot would destroy his face and probably kill him. There would be blood all over the place, and she would wash her hands in it, rub it on her arms and face, revel in the joy of revenge for the death of a creature far more valuable than Robert Beekman could ever dream of being.

It wouldn't be necessary to give the bird human traits to take pleasure in killing its killer. The bird was dead, but she was alive. The vengeance would be hers alone.

The vision of Robert Beekman's face dissolving into shattered bone and blood played out behind her closed eyelids. When it was over, she realized she was gritting her teeth so hard they hurt, and so did her clenched, arthritic fists. She relaxed her jaw and her fingers slowly to allow the cramped muscles and aching joints to ease back to their usual level of pain.

It had been more than 30 years since she'd last camped out, when her two youngest boys were in their early teens. She'd been a lot stronger then and far more agile, and they'd stayed in campgrounds with toilets and showers. This adventure would be much different. That she, too, was much different only made it more daunting.

She had enough trouble sleeping in her own bed. Nights spent in a sleeping bag with only a thin mat between her aching body and the ground didn't seem like a formula for comfortable rest. As for nourishment, she'd eaten freeze-dried food once out of curiosity. It wasn't terrible, but it wasn't the kind of thing anyone would want to live on. Certainly nothing like croissants from the Double Dyke Bakery or toast with butter and strawberry jam. But it would do, and all she needed was one pot and some water to make a meal. Where she was headed, the water in the creek would be clean enough to drink, so she wouldn't have to carry it.

What most concerned her was navigating the rough terrain. She'd have to be careful because she couldn't trust her strength or her balance. A fall could be catastrophic, especially with no one knowing where she was.

The more she thought about it, the more the whole thing seemed like a fool's errand. The odds of finding another new bird were far worse than those of winding up dead from exposure or injury. Yet the craziness only made her more determined to take the challenge on. If no one ever saw her again, the only thing she'd lose was the opportunity to molder beside her husband in a small-town cemetery. It seemed like a small price to pay.

Having a plan of action relieved the grief and sadness that had weighed on her since Beekman killed the bird and drove off with her sense of purpose sealed in a plastic bag and shut up in an ice chest. It also allowed her to use her hatred of Beekman and her anger at what he'd done to drive her. She fed on those feelings to give her the energy she needed to take back her discovery.

How she would take it back, even if she found another new bird, she didn't know. Beekman was the ornithologist, the expert. She was just an old lady living in a tiny town in Colorado, watching birds in her yard. He had the bird in hand, so to speak. All she could do was prove to the world that more of the new birds existed by finding them and photographing them herself. To trust anyone else to help her seemed the height of foolishness. Not even Janet had been reliable. Protests aside, Janet's trustworthiness was questionable. She couldn't be sure Janet hadn't said something to Matt or Sheriff MacGregor or both and covered it up by pretending to be hurt. No, Janet was out of the picture. She was on her own now.

Looking back, she realized trusting people had never been easy for her. There were just too many reasons not to count on them. She loved Ed, but she had to admit she hadn't trusted him entirely. Now, although she couldn't prove it, she thought her lack of faith in him had been earned. She was sure he'd had an affair.

Even the person she considered her best friend — maybe only friend — in the world couldn't be relied on to tell her the truth. Milly Brewster died without ever telling her she wasn't well. What an awful thing to do. Then another, unwelcome thought struck her. What if Milly hadn't trusted her? What if Milly thought she couldn't take the news, would fall apart? No. Milly knew better. After all, if anything could shatter her, it would be Ed's death, and she'd survived that. Milly had betrayed her.

People hid things. They lied. They talked about other people behind their back. They faked their emotions, putting on an act to cover their real feelings. They pretended to love each other, all the while concealing their resentments and disdain. Always there was an ulterior motive, a desire for something the other person would not give willingly, something too much.

She had been fooled too often to believe people could be trusted. Robert Beekman and Janet had been the latest examples. If she failed to return from the mountains, if she died trying to find the new bird alive, it would be far better than giving her life over to some caretaker in a few years. The thought of living long enough to reach a point where she was unable to care for herself scared her more than death. No matter who her caretaker might be — whether family member or hired hand — she knew she couldn't trust that she would be treated with honesty, kindness, and respect.

Some people might call her paranoid, but she knew better. She'd experienced the truth too many times. Human beings were fucking assholes.

While she sat musing, the sun had gone down. The room had darkened, and the moon lit her feeders. The birds had long since abandoned them to find a roosting place for the night. A bobcat ran across the yard, seeking water from the creek, most likely. She had seen black bears out there, the cubs walking up to the windows and looking in. Mule deer were frequent visitors, their outsized ears twisting to pick up every sound. Once, a mountain lion had slinked under the feeders, its flat head close to the ground and its tail floating just above it. The big cat paid no attention to her, apparently confident in its ability to tear her apart if she were stupid enough to step outside.

She could trust the animals and birds, at least. The fact that they didn't give a damn about her unless she posed a threat comforted her. She knew where she stood with them. Without turning on a light or getting anything to eat, she went to bed, falling asleep to the creek's rumbling lullaby more quickly than usual.

ELEVEN

O n Thursday, she knew, Sheriff MacGregor would come by to make sure she was still among the living and not in dire straits of one kind or another. It was part of his routine to visit the town's old folks on a regular schedule. The timing worked well for her. Her supplies and equipment would arrive by Friday. She'd leave on Saturday, and the sheriff wouldn't come by again for two weeks. By then, she'd either be back at home or dead.

Thursday morning, she spent a few hours cleaning the house. She didn't want the sheriff thinking she'd stopped taking care of the place. Admittedly, it needed a good going over. Dust had accumulated on every surface, and the laundry had piled up. She didn't use the second bathroom, so it was fine, but hers was a mess, the toilet and sink both dirty and the tub sporting a brownish-gray ring. By the time she finished scrubbing and dusting, the house looked presentable.

Housekeeping had never been something she enjoyed, and her arthritis and sore shoulder made it akin to torture. She took a bath in her clean tub to ease the pain and make sure she smelled all right.

As usual, Sheriff MacGregor showed up around 1:00 in the afternoon. He knocked on the front door, and she met him there, wearing fresh clothing, her hair washed and combed. He stepped inside.

"How's everything going?"

"Healthy as a horse and happy as a clam."

He smiled. "Glad to hear it. Any problems?" As he spoke, his eyes wandered around the room.

"Nothing at all, except aches and pains. Not anything to be concerned about."

"Okay, then." He turned, pushed the storm door open and stepped out onto the porch. "Guess I'll be going."

"Thanks for stopping by."

He tipped his cowboy hat and walked down the stairs to his car. She closed the door, stepped back into the shadows and watched him through the window. He scanned the yard, probably looking for any signs that she wasn't taking care of the place or following her regular habits and routines. Then he stepped into his patrol car and drove away down the lane.

Relieved, she walked to the kitchen and drew a glass of water from the tap. Only two formalities left before she could get away without any hint of what she was up to, and they both would happen the next day. She had to meet Janet at the bakery, and Sheriff MacGregor and Matt were sure to be there, too. UPS or FedEx would deliver her camping gear and camera as well. She doubted all the stuff would come at the same time. She only knew that everything was scheduled to be delivered tomorrow.

UPS and FedEx trucks were a common sight in Valley View. Most of the people who lived there, at least the older ones, didn't want to drive 100 miles round trip to the nearest decent shopping. The trucks shouldn't draw too much attention.

After drinking a large glass of water, she felt a little sloshy, so she sat at the table to let her body absorb the liquid. Her stomach growled, and she realized she hadn't eaten anything all day. She'd gone right to work cleaning house without making her coffee and toast with butter and strawberry jam. It surprised her that she'd forgotten her breakfast, but it was probably because she was anxious about the sheriff's visit and wanted to be sure the place was ready.

The sheriff's inspection brought up something she'd failed to consider — how she might be found out before she completed her mission in the mountains. Sheriff MacGregor wouldn't be back for two weeks, so he wasn't a problem. The biggest threat came from Janet. The snoop might take it upon herself to check the house.

She couldn't think of anything that would give her away except the Blazer in the garage. She would have to hike to the trailhead from her house and leave the car at home. Leaving it near the trail would be entirely too risky. On the other hand, if Janet noticed it, she'd be worried and probably call the sheriff to break into the house to make sure there was no dead body. The garage would be locked, of course, but there was a side door with a small window. Something would have to be done about that.

She got up and found a hammer in the toolbox she kept in the hall closet along with some good-sized nails she had in a box on the shelf. She walked to the garage and gathered some scrap lumber left over when she'd had the bridge across the creek rebuilt the summer before. Choosing five pieces she thought were long enough, she carried them to the door. With considerable effort, she nailed the planks to the window frame, one on top of the other until the entire opening was covered so no one could see in or tell that the glass remained intact. Satisfied, she carried the hammer and nails back into the house and put them away.

She'd have to come up with a story to explain the covered window and a way to make sure Janet didn't take it upon herself to get it fixed. That part was easy enough. It took only a few minutes to concoct a tale she thought would do the job.

She turned her attention to the birds on and around the feeders, hoping she'd been wrong about there being just one new one. Only the regulars were present — chickadees, nuthatches, Steller's jays, magpies and, on the ground, juncos. The empty space where the new bird's favorite feeder used to be seemed huge. She would need to fill it soon to remove the reminder of how stupid she'd been and how much her stupidity had cost.

Her stomach rumbled again. She walked to the kitchen and put the tea kettle on to heat. While she prepared her toast and jam, she paused often to look out the window at the creek. It was only May, so the weather was still chilly. It would be much colder where she was going. The snow receded slowly at the higher elevations, but it was melting. The creek had grown wider and noisier since she'd taken her fall. The water roiled and sent up spray as it crashed against the larger boulders.

Most years, she and Ed — and the boys when they were still around — spent a few days during the Christmas holidays in Valley View. The house had no furnace or any other source of heat except the fireplace and a wood-burning stove. They had no bathroom and used an outhouse about 50 yards down an unpaved path. Water came from a well via a handpump. Electricity was the one modern convenience.

Often, the snow cover extended from the peaks to the valley, creating a brown-gray-white landscape consisting of vast fields of snow, punctuated with leafless cottonwoods along the streams, bare-limbed aspen in large and smaller patches on the mountainsides and different species of conifers in various shades of green. Wind sweeping the ragged peaks created horizontal plumes, stripping the crags of snow and leaving the gray rock revealed.

The effect was both haunting and beautiful — in daylight, forbidding, at sunrise and sunset glorious in reds and yellows, at night under a sky layered deep with stars, both intimidating and oddly intimate. It was a landscape that kept its distance, yet, when she was alone in it, held her in its embrace.

No matter how cold it got, the creek flowed, the water moving too fast to freeze completely. A sheet of ice would form, enough to hold a layer of snow, but the sound of water rolling over the rocks beneath never ceased.

When the boys were young, she and Ed would take them to Valley View for at least two weeks in the summer. Sometimes, she and the boys would stay for six weeks or more while Ed returned to work. She missed him when he left but not because of the support he gave her in keeping the kids clean, clothed, and fed and the house livable. Ed believed in maintaining clearly separate roles, circumstances be damned. Anything having to do with keeping house was her responsibility. He seemed to see the arrangement as so obviously right that he gave it no thought.

She told herself, when she considered it, that he worked hard and deserved to relax. He shouldn't have to worry about cooking and cleaning when he was on vacation. So she said nothing. She only wished she had more time to spend with him when his work didn't consume him.

Summers in Valley View started with swarms of mosquitoes that made life miserable until mid-July when they suddenly disappeared. After that, the family could enjoy the cool nights and warm days with afternoon thunderstorms that left the air sweet with the scent of wet piñon pine and juniper. The creek, of course, rumbled and crashed with snowmelt early in the season and then settled down to a duller roar in July and August.

With the boys in tow, she and Ed would hike the trails through the national forest to the timberline lakes that fed the streams. Ed always had his camera on a tripod slung over his shoulder, putting it down when he spotted a bird and trying to get the perfect shot. The boys learned to swear on those hikes, getting graphic lessons whenever a bird flew too soon.

The scream of the tea kettle brought her back from her reverie. She turned the stove off, got the bread, jam and butter from the refrigerator and placed them on the counter.

Something was missing, though. She studied the items she placed on the counter but couldn't decide what wasn't there that should be. Everything seemed out of order, confusing. For several minutes, she stood and tried to figure out what was wrong. Then, leaving the tea kettle sitting on the burner, she made her toast and jam, carried it to the table and started eating. After the first bite, she reached for her mug of coffee. It wasn't there. Then she realized what was missing. She hadn't made her instant coffee.

Nothing strange about that. She'd strayed from her usual routine. With the steps out of order, she could be expected to leave something out. The water was still hot, so she made her coffee and returned to the table to finish her meal.

After eating, she put her dishes in the dishwasher and, noting that it was full, added detergent and started it. The day's work had left her exhausted, but she was happy to note that her shoulder hurt much less. She should be able to carry the backpack with minimal discomfort, as long as it wasn't too heavy. She ran another glass of water, drank it all and sat in her recliner to watch TV.

When she woke, it was dark. On the television, a sitcom played, the canned laughter annoyingly raucous and loud. She turned the set off, paid her visit to the bathroom and went to bed.

Friday morning, she didn't awaken until almost 9:00. Her body hurt more than usual, probably because of the cleaning she'd done in preparation for the sheriff's visit and the lifting, holding and hammering she had to do to hide the Blazer. She crawled out of bed, put on her robe and slippers and made her customary breakfast, this time remembering to prepare the coffee because she followed the steps.

By 10:00, she was dressed and ready to head for the Double Dyke Bakery for her croissant and to finish setting up the smoke screen that would hide her intentions for the next ten days. The challenge of the subterfuge excited and scared her, but what she most looked forward to was the pastry. It would be her last, possibly forever, so she wanted to enjoy it.

She stepped outside into a light, chilly drizzle that she hoped would end before tomorrow, when she would begin her journey on foot. A few minutes later, she was walking into the bakery, her nose filled with the scent of fresh pastries and coffee.

Janet, Matt and Sheriff MacGregor were already at a table, and they'd saved a fourth chair for her. After exchanging greetings, she started to order her coffee and croissant from Minnie, who raised her hand to stop her.

"One plain croissant . . ."

Tilly chimed in, ". . . with a side of strawberry jam and one coffee . . ."

" . . . coming right up," Minnie said.

The way these two finished each other's sentences would certainly be annoying after a while, but in small doses she had to admit it was rather charming. She returned Minnie's smile and thanked her, nodding her gratitude to Tilly as well.

When she sat down, the other three people at the table were quiet. She took advantage of the lull in the conversation to build her cover story.

"A magpie flew into my garage window yesterday and broke it."

Janet looked concerned. "It must have hit the glass awfully hard. Was it okay?"

"It staggered around a bit but then flew off like nothing happened."

"Well, I hope the bird is okay."

"I'm sure it'll be fine. I went ahead and boarded up the window. I'll get it fixed when I come back from my trip. I'll put some of those stickers on the glass that keep birds from flying into it."

Sheriff MacGregor, apparently unfazed by her story, said, "I understand you're going to visit the kids."

"All of them, in fact. I figure it'll take about two weeks. I'll be leaving as early as I can tomorrow."

Janet, always the inquisitive reporter, said, "That's not much time to visit five families in how many states?"

"Five, but one of them is Colorado."

"With all the driving, that doesn't give you much time with each one."

"A day or so is plenty. I don't want to put them out."

"That's barely enough time to say hello and goodbye."

"I don't wear well."

Matt said, "I don't believe that."

"I don't either," Janet said. "You're the model of sweetness and light."

Matt snorted at that but covered it fairly well. Helen decided to play it for a laugh to ease the tension and change the subject.

"No. I'm difficult, irascible, sometimes downright nasty, and I won't have it any other way. So there."

A long pause ensued, then Sheriff MacGregor laughed. Everyone followed his lead, even Tilly and Minnie. Helen grinned. Mission accomplished.

Tilly delivered her croissant and coffee. She took a bite of pastry after adding a little jam. It was wonderful. Lying seemed to enhance her sense of taste.

Through the window, she saw a UPS truck pass, heading toward her house. She hoped it carried part of what she'd ordered. Matt followed her gaze and spotted the truck.

"Expecting something?"

"No, no. I don't order much. I like to shop the old-fashioned way, in a store."

That was true. But finding what she needed for her mission would have taken too long the old-fashioned way. It was easier to search the magazine ads and order by phone. There was also little chance anyone would see what she was buying and wonder why she was purchasing camping equipment. It was unlikely, but she couldn't take any chances.

Anxious to get back to see what might be left on her front porch, she tried not to eat faster than usual. The croissant tasted so good, but she was ready to go. She'd planted her deceptions well. She didn't want to take a chance on saying something that might cause suspicion or maybe even give her away. She let the others talk and focused on keeping her mouth full so she couldn't join in.

As soon as she took her last bite of pastry and sip of coffee, she said, "I have to go. Packing to do," and stood up. She swayed a little, and Matt caught her arm to steady her.

"I'm fine." It came out a little testier than she'd intended. Matt looked hurt as he let her go.

She tried to make light of the moment. She smiled at Matt. "Sorry. Like I said, I can be downright nasty."

He smiled back, seeming to understand. She touched his shoulder, said goodbye to all of them, waved to Tilly and Minnie, and left.

When she got home, a box waited for her on her front porch. Once inside, she put it on the table and opened it, feeling like she once had on her birthday or at Christmas. Beneath the plastic air pillows, she found her new camera, packaged in cardboard and Styrofoam, safe from anything short of a nuclear blast. Her excitement somewhat diminished, she withdrew the camera from the carton and set it aside. A second box held her 200-600mm lens. This instrument she laid gently beside the camera, afraid of doing any damage to what she thought must be a delicate piece of equipment.

For the first time since all things digital — a word she'd learned from Janet that seemed to cover everything that wasn't normal — destroyed the world, she wished she knew more about how to make the damned gizmos work. Her new camera terrified her, but she knew she had to learn how to use it. So she sat down at the table and started poring over the instructions.

Three hours later, she thought she might have some idea how to take pictures with a camera that had no film. Apparently, a tiny card could hold an unbelievable number of images, and she could see them as soon as she took them, just by pushing a button. She had to admit that not having to wait for developed photos to come back before she could see whether they were any good was a plus.

The thing even focused itself. She tried pointing it at a birdfeeder where a mountain chickadee pecked at thistle seed, and the blurry bird became crystal clear almost instantly without her touching anything. The picture she took looked good, too, although the bird seemed too small. She tried again, using the zoom button to bring the image closer, and the results pleased her.

She heard a vehicle roll up to the porch. She walked down the hall as heavy footsteps sounded on the porch stairs and looked out the window beside the front door. A UPS van sat in the driveway. Someone knocked, but she didn't answer, preferring to let the driver leave the delivery and go away. Soon, she heard footsteps descending the stairs. The van departed.

She opened the front door to find several more packages. It looked like everything besides the camera had arrived at the same time. Back at the table, a quick check of the opened boxes confirmed her guess. This was good. The fewer delivery vehicles the better. She pulled out the tent, boots, sleeping bag and pad, cook set, flashlight, and freeze-dried food, and spread them on her bed, along with the other gear she'd ordered.

Seeing her equipment and supplies arrayed in front of her brought back the times when, as a young girl, she'd longed to be an explorer. She'd wanted to be part of an expedition to discover things no other human being had ever seen. Watching her mother grow more and more timid, until she feared leaving the house, strengthened her desire to explore beyond the narrow confines of her life. She read everything she could find about men — they were all men, of course — who traveled all over the world, advancing knowledge and, apparently, having a lot of fun.

But her life remained confined. The effort to break away by going to college ended with Ed. She hadn't had the will to resist her desires and the pull of tradition, so she'd married him. As a result, he had the adventures while she stayed home with the children.

The only time she'd made a break for something more — and it was a modest something — was when she went back to college. It wasn't exactly an expedition to the Amazon, but her forays to the wetland gave her something of the sense of wonder and discovery she'd longed for in her youth. She never knew what she'd find each time she went. It might be an unusual bird, blown off-course by a storm, a plant she hadn't seen before, or an insect, or a nest of eggs or hatchlings. Anticipation got her out of bed each morning and sent her to bed each night looking forward to the next day. She had been something akin to happy for the first ten months of her project.

Then Beekman had turned from prince to ogre, and the joy she'd felt in her work dissolved into shame and anger. Anger at his seemingly unwarranted attack and shame at her failure to react with courage — to defend herself. Now, many years after that day at the wetland, she still lacked the fortitude to confront him the way she thought she should.

She took a deep breath and threw her shoulders back, causing her arthritis to remind her she shouldn't make sudden moves. This time, though, the pain only served to lend power to her resolve. The anger might remain, but the shame had to go. She would prove what kind of woman she was.

She took the time to figure out how to set up the tent. It was easier than she expected. It just popped into shape. All she had to do was stake it down.

Sitting at the table, she reviewed her preparations to make sure she hadn't overlooked anything. She had all the food and equipment she thought she needed. The Blazer was safely hidden behind a locked garage door and a boarded-over window. Tonight, she'd fill her backpack, including a couple of bottles of water to hold her until she got far enough up the mountain to trust water from the creek and the many springs along the trail.

Tomorrow morning, before the sun had fully risen, she'd set out. It would be easiest to reach the trailhead by walking on the road, but she couldn't risk that. Instead, she would follow the creek north, using the narrow trail meant for anglers in pursuit of trout. The first leg of her hike would test her, she knew. She couldn't wait to get started.

That night, she slept in fragments, waking from the same dream that seemed to proceed like a movie with gaps in the film. She had a hard time following it because it didn't flow like a story, even the kind of bizarre narrative dreams usually played out. In one segment, she saw the new bird at its favorite feeder explode into a cloud of feathers and blood. In another, she was holding it, dead but apparently in one piece. In between, Beekman screamed at her, telling her she wasn't who she should be. Then Ed was there, standing by, saying nothing as Beekman berated her. Just before she gave up on sleeping and climbed out of bed, she dreamed that Beekman exploded in front of her, showering her in blood and pieces of flesh and bone.

The dream disturbed her, not because of Beekman's fantasy demise but because she took such delight in it. She frowned but felt like smiling as she put on warm clothes and fixed her breakfast of toast and coffee.

When she opened the refrigerator to retrieve the butter and jam, she found her new camera sitting on the shelf. She stared at it, wondering how on earth it got there. She must have absent-mindedly put it in the refrigerator while she was thinking about something else or done it in her sleep. She couldn't remember opening the refrigerator at all the night before. It was strange, but she dismissed it, put the camera on the table and went back to fixing her breakfast.

After eating, she lifted the backpack onto her shoulders and fastened the strap around her waist. The thing was heavy, but she could carry it. She tried walking around the room a few times, testing her legs. Each step sent shocks of pain from her shoulders to her ankles, but she could manage the hurt. It might be worse on the uneven ground she'd have to navigate. She'd just have to take it slow.

It had been dark when she got out of bed. Now the light had begun to grow and reveal fog and a light mist. This wasn't good. She checked the thermometer hanging outside the east window. Thirty-nine degrees. So it shouldn't be icy. If it were, she'd still go, but it would be dangerous. As it was, the moisture on the wooden bridge over the creek as well as the rocks along the trail would make them slippery.

Time to leave. Still carrying the backpack, she checked the lock on the front door and left through the back, taking the stairs down to the creekside with both hands on the railing, putting both feet on each step before moving on.

At the bridge, she held on to both railings and stepped slowly across. Her new boots seemed to give her feet more purchase, and she made the crossing without incident.

On the east side of the creek, she turned north, following the almost invisible fishing trail. The damp and cold penetrated to her skin, and she shivered, suddenly realizing she'd forgotten her stocking cap, coat and gloves. She would have to go back to the house and start all over again. How she'd gotten this far without noticing she had no idea. The walk back went smoothly, though, and she was soon back on the trail after adjusting the straps on her backpack to accommodate the bulk of her coat.

She checked her watch. It was 7:30, and the light was getting stronger despite the mist and fog. If she walked slowly and deliberately, keeping her eyes on the path, she figured she'd be fine. This trek would take a while, but she had the time.

The air, fragrant with pine, birch, and damp earth, gave her incentive to keep moving. She wasn't used to so much humidity and, despite her sweater and coat, she felt the cold. In spite of the pain in her back, shoulders and legs, she was happy to be outside and moving under her own power. She was glad no one knew where she was, and she wasn't expecting to meet anyone who knew her. Anonymity freed her.

Anonymity also scared her a little, but she fought the fear. What if she fell and hurt herself or a mountain lion attacked her, and no one could find her? There were worse things, she told herself, than freezing to death in these woods and being consumed by its animals, birds and, ultimately, worms, bugs, and bacteria.

She checked her watch again. Only 30 minutes had passed since her second departure from home. A boulder offered her a place to rest, and she accepted.

An American raven's deep double croak broke the silence. The big, black birds often circled the ridges above her, along with turkey vultures, in search of dead things or anything else to eat. She had a soft spot for ravens and vultures, but especially ravens. Vultures lacked the beauty and elegance of other raptors, what with their featherless red heads that prevented the carrion they fed on from sticking to their skin, but when they soared, riding rising thermals, they were majestic. As for ravens, they seemed unafraid and bold, demanding their due from life, and they let their voice be heard.

The mist had left a film on her face and droplets on her eyelashes. She pulled a tissue from her coat pocket and mopped her face then returned it, even though it was shredded. She pushed herself up from her seat on the boulder and almost toppled over because of the still unfamiliar weight of the backpack. With her right hand, she grabbed a cottonwood sapling and managed to halt what could have been a disastrous tumble onto rocks half-buried in the soil.

She cried out, "God damn son of a bitch." It was Ed's favorite curse, one he used as a catch-all when things didn't go his way. If he missed a shot on the tennis court, or something fell on his foot, or a bird flew too soon to catch it in a photo, he'd go to "God damn son of a bitch" without a second thought.

But why did it come so naturally to her now? It had flown out of her mouth. And it seemed exactly the right thing to say, not because it meant anything but because it was as coarse as the pain in her shoulder. It was a kind of homeopathic remedy. She used it to fight fire with fire.

"It was all a mistake."

Her curse still echoed when the words came again. She heard them in the voice of Robert Beekman.

She turned in the direction of the sound, and there he was, standing with his binoculars and camera dangling from his neck and a shotgun tucked under his right arm. In his left hand, he held the carcass of the new bird. He was smiling.

"You're fucking right it was all a mistake, you asshole," she said, her voice low and tight. "A mistake that will cost you your reputation. I know how much you wanted to be at the top of your field. You never made it, and you won't make it with my bird."

Still smiling, Beekman disappeared. Strangely, his sudden appearance and vanishing failed to frighten her. She knew he couldn't have been where he was, yet it seemed as natural as her ability to curse and her anger. The only thing that bothered her was that smile. No matter how insulting her words might be, they couldn't wipe that fucking smile off his face. That was all it took to give him the victory.

She yelled at the space Beekman had occupied seconds before. "Come back here, you bastard." He left her standing there, fuming at a rocky hillside dotted with piñons, junipers, prickly pear cactus, and yucca. A raven croaked its double "caw," from somewhere above her in the fog. Tears trickled down her cheeks, which were already wet again from the mist. She pulled the tattered tissue from her pocket, wiped the tears away and started walking, trying to focus on the path.

Years ago, in a time that seemed so near, she'd been able to hike without always looking down. She'd kept her eyes up, watching for soaring hawks and eagles as well as smaller birds sitting on branches or flitting from tree to tree. But her body had betrayed her, and it made her mad.

She'd been pretty when she was young, but that hardly mattered now that she wasn't anymore. It wasn't her beauty she missed but her strength and agility. What had once been easy now wasn't. Climbing stairs, getting in and out of cars, rising from bed or standing up from a chair — all had become physical challenges. Worst of all was the feeling of instability, the constant threat of losing her balance as she had the other day when she'd hurt her shoulder. That anyone had to go through such a loss of function seemed to her an outrage.

Of course, she knew aging occurred naturally and had its natural consequences as the body wore out. When it happened to her, though, it seemed unfair. It happened too soon and came on so fast. At least, it felt that way. Had it really been ten years since she'd last played tennis? That final time on the court had been torture. She'd struggled to run down the ball and scraped her knee badly when her left leg gave out and she fell. Her opponent, a younger woman whose name she couldn't recall, had run to her side and helped her up. The humiliation, more than anything, led her to quit playing.

Now here she was, stumbling along a fishing path, eyes glued to the ground, trying to stay upright and already feeling bone-weary. She couldn't have walked more than a mile, probably much less, yet her legs trembled and her shoulders ached as though she'd hiked the eight miles to Darkling Lake and back. She would have to rest again soon, but she was determined to go a little farther before stopping.

A glance at her watch told her she'd been on the trail for five hours. A few years ago, that much time walking would have been enough to put her at the trailhead at least three hours ago. She knew she still had a long way to go, thanks to frequent and lengthy rest stops. For another 15 minutes, she walked as fast as her weakening legs could carry her.

When she found a boulder large enough to let her half-sit, she took off her backpack. Removing the weight from her shoulders felt so good, she laughed with relief and shrugged, a movement that turned her laugh into a groan as her right shoulder protested.

She rubbed her shoulder and looked around. The mist had stopped, and the fog had lifted. She wanted to turn around and look at the ridge above her to see if she could get her bearings. She had walked the road to the trailhead many times and was familiar with the ridge's changing shape. She would do it if she could work up the energy, but she couldn't move. All she wanted was a long sleep.

The only benefit of her exhaustion was its numbing effect. Little of the pain she lived with every day affected her as she sat on the boulder and stared at the creek.

Eventually, she forced herself to stand and turn around so she could view the ridge. It looked different than it did from the road, and she didn't see anything familiar in the rugged terrain. She'd just have to keep going until she couldn't move anymore. The way she felt, that point wouldn't be long coming.

Lifting the backpack onto her shoulders sapped what strength she had left, so she leaned against the boulder to rest. Would it be so bad to give up now? She could quit the way she did when she left college to marry Ed and try another time when she felt better. And when would that be? Would she wait 30 years the way she had before? That kind of time no longer existed for her. She had to do this now or die knowing she not only failed but hadn't really tried. It wouldn't be bad to quit now. It would be the worst thing she'd ever done.

Pushing herself away from the boulder's support, she turned north again and took a few shaky, tentative steps. Not so bad. She hadn't collapsed. She could make it a little farther, at least. When she could, she used boulders and tree branches to help keep her upright. In between those supports, she moved forward with small steps, halting often to wait for her legs to stop quivering. What progress she made came with frustrating slowness. She thought if anyone saw her, they'd think she'd been drinking, something she wouldn't mind doing at the moment. A scotch and water would be nice.

She'd given up booze after Ed had his stroke. Over the years, a little scotch mixed with lots of water had been a comfort to her, especially after the boys all left to live their lives elsewhere.

When Tony went off to college, the house felt empty. She'd rattled around in the big place after Ed left for work in the morning, trying to find something to do and sipping scotch and water until it soothed her into not caring that all she had to occupy her was cooking and cleaning.

She tried substitute teaching but found high school students irritating and frustrating. She'd raised five of them. That was enough. It was time to find something else to do besides catering to spoiled teenagers.

So she stayed home, kept house and sipped scotch and water, never drinking enough to be obvious but just the right amount to give her that pleasant floaty feeling. It helped her avoid thinking about Ed's retirement and how it wouldn't happen because Ed didn't want it to.

No matter how often she talked to him about remodeling the house in Valley View and settling down there, he refused to make plans. After a while, she changed tactics. Instead of pressing him about retiring to Colorado, she tried appealing to his love of travel, a fondness she didn't share, sending off for brochures with pictures of beautiful motor homes. At first, he seemed interested. Before long, though, he wouldn't discuss travel or motor homes or the house in Valley View.

She decided to let the matter rest for a while instead of pushing Ed to make a decision. The delay probably was for the best. It wasn't long before he began to show signs of mental deterioration, forgetting things and repeating himself. Had they bought the motor home, it would have sat unused until she sold it at what would have probably been a big loss.

The house was a different story. It didn't matter that they might not move there permanently. It still needed remodeling. Walking to the outhouse no longer seemed like an adventure. It had become a pain, especially in the winter. Indoor plumbing was essential. So was a decent stove. She would not live like a pioneer woman anymore, not even for a two-week vacation.

The work went on as Ed's condition worsened. By the time he had his stroke, the bulk of the construction was finished. She added a wheelchair ramp in case he wouldn't walk again. Ed progressed rather steadily for six months, getting to the point where he could walk short distances with a cane, go to the bathroom and bathe himself. His mind had cleared as well, so they could carry on a fairly coherent conversation. She figured they'd be ready to move by around a year after the stroke, in April or May.

When she was honest with herself, she had to admit that, no matter how hard it had been to bring Ed back to some semblance of his old self, his stroke had in many ways given her what she wanted. He could no longer practice medicine. His cognitive abilities had been damaged too much. Retirement was no longer a choice. Although his behavior tended to be erratic, with sudden outbursts of anger and aggressive sexual advances, he was, for the most part, docile and compliant. She would have little trouble putting him in the car and taking him to Valley View. Thanks to her son's help, the house would be ready for him when they arrived.

Then, of course, the second stroke finished what the first had begun, and she had made the move by herself. As sad as she felt walking into a new home that Ed would never see, she also experienced a sense of freedom that was entirely novel. Never in her life had she had no one looking over her shoulder, judging her for what she did and didn't do. She believed the sadness would never leave her — it would be wrong if it did — but the joy of liberation tempered it.

Remembering stepping into her house that first day seemed to give her new energy. She picked up her pace a bit, her legs feeling stronger, her breathing easier. Her right shoulder hurt her a little less, and the rest of her aches and pains had eased.

For a half hour or so, she made relatively good time, but evening, brought on before its time by the cloud cover, made it difficult to see obstacles that could trip her. It had taken her nine hours to walk perhaps a mile, but she had to stop. The danger of trying to go on outweighed her enthusiasm for reaching her goal. She would have to make camp where she stood.

Where to begin? She would need to boil any water she took from the creek. All day, she'd sipped from the bottles she'd packed. The second one was almost empty. She'd need more to drink and cook. So the first order of business was building a fire. She slipped out of the backpack and started gathering rocks, which she placed to form a circle. The effort took all her energy.

Before gathering wood, she sat on a boulder to rest. It took a long time for her to gather enough strength to search for dry grass and twigs to start the blaze and larger pieces of piñon to feed it.

Once she'd made a small pile of shredded cottonwood bark, she lit it with one of the matches she'd almost forgotten to pack and watched as the flames caught. She fed the small fire with twigs until yellow tongues shot up a foot or so into the air. Choosing a few larger piñon sticks, she laid them on the briskly burning fire and retired to her boulder seat.

The crackling and fragrance of burning piñon, along with the warmth of the fire, provided a refuge from the cold near darkness surrounding her. Beyond the ring of light, she could hear the creek bounding downhill.

She would need the flashlight to get to the water and fill her bottles. She found it and the bottles in her backpack and used the beam to guide her to the creek side about 30 feet beyond the farthest reach of the firelight. Kneeling to reach the water hurt her knees and her back, and she could feel the splash-wet moss soaking her pants. But she got two full bottles of water and carried them back to her campsite.

After putting some more wood on the fire, she found two forked sticks, used her new hand ax to trim them and tried to push them into the earth on either side of the fireplace she'd fashioned. The rocky soil wouldn't let her sink them more than an inch or so, no matter where she tried. Frustrated, she looked for another solution.

Soon, the obvious answer came to her. The rocks. There were plenty of them. She built two towers of stones to a height she deemed adequate. Then she found the cook-set in her backpack and filled the largest pot with water. This she hung on a stick supported by the stone towers and spanning the fire.

While she waited for the water to boil, she pulled her tent out and laid it on a patch of sandy ground. It did what it was supposed to do, popped into shape in an instant. She pounded the stakes into the sand with a rock and spread her sleeping pad and bag inside.

Back at the fire, the water boiled. She'd give it a few more minutes to make sure it was safe and then fix herself some dinner while she boiled some more to drink.

Hunger made her feel almost sick. She had to eat or she might pass out. In the backpack, she found a package of dehydrated beef stroganoff. After giving the boiling water another couple of minutes, she dumped the stroganoff into a smaller pot and poured in the boiling water. The stuff actually smelled good, and she started eating before it was fully hydrated. She added a little hot water and stirred the concoction before taking another mouthful. When she finished eating, she was still hungry, but she felt better. She added wood to the fire, used more of the hot water to clean the pot she'd eaten from and put more water in the larger pot to boil. That much clean water should give her enough for the next day.

In the darkness beyond the firelight, she could hear animals searching for food. She wished she had something to give them, but she knew that would invite them to the campsite. Bears were in the area, and they would have smelled her stroganoff cooking. She found the smaller cookpot and a metal spoon and kept them close by her side.

A long time ago, she'd experienced a bear visit. When she and Ed and the two youngest boys were camping in Shenandoah National Park, two black bears tore their ice chest to pieces while they stood by helplessly, afraid of attracting the big animals' attention by screaming and waving their arms. Then she remembered a nature program she'd seen on television. A woman had chased a black bear away by banging on a skillet with a wooden spoon. She decided to give it a try and ran to the fire, dumped the contents of a skillet on the ground and used a serving spoon to bang away at it.

It worked. Both bears left the scene. From that point on, she kept the skillet and spoon within easy reach. For their part, the bears never returned, and the message must have gotten out, because no other bears came looking for dinner.

Remembering the ancient incident with the bears reminded her that she should hang her pack well off the ground for the night to keep it out of reach of prowling animals. She had packed a long piece of rope for the purpose but wasn't sure she had the strength to toss it up and over a limb that was high enough. She had to try, though. The rest of her mission depended on it. She couldn't afford to lose her food and other supplies.

Taking the rope from her pack, she found a cottonwood with a stout limb far enough up to put the pack out of reach. She threw the coiled rope as hard as she could, but it fell well short of its target. She tried again and again and twice more before her arm hurt so badly she had to stop for a rest.

This approach was not working. She needed something besides her muscle power to send the rope high enough to curl over the limb. Searching the ground, she found an oblong stone she deemed large and heavy enough to do the job, if her aim was good.

After tying the rope to the stone, she coiled most of it on the ground in front of her, holding the end not tied to the stone in her left hand. Then she started swinging the stone in a circle, widening it until the stone almost hit the ground. At the top of her last swing, she released the rope in her right hand. The stone sailed up and over the limb and hit the ground a few feet in front of her. She'd done it.

The stub of a broken limb stuck out from the tree's trunk about six feet off the ground. She tied the end of the rope she held in her left hand to it and wound the rope around the stub until she'd removed all the slack. Then she replaced the stone with her pack. The rest was just a matter of pulling on the rope to raise the pack high enough so it was safe and tying it off on the stub.

Worn out but happy with her success, she returned to the fire, removed the boiling water and set it aside to let it cool. It would soon be ready to put in the bottles.

For a while, she sat by the fire, watching it burn down to coals and breathing the scent of piñon smoke rising into the night sky. As the circle of light contracted, she could see the reach of stars across the sky more clearly. The immensity of it never failed to put her in awe.

Far up on the mountainside, a mountain lion screamed, and she pulled her jacket closer around her shoulders. She would put some more wood on the fire before she turned in, just in case the mountain lion got curious. She wasn't sure it was true that mountain lions feared fire, but she liked the idea.

She had spent many nights alone and had long since become comforttable with darkness. But most of those nights — in fact, all of them for the past 25 years — had been spent indoors in a bed. Tonight, she felt not just alone but exposed. For a moment, she longed for the security of solid walls around her. The flimsy material of her tent could not protect her from much of anything except light rain.

Then she remembered why she was where she was. Her eyes moved from the small fire in front of her to the myriad tiny fires above her, knowing they were tiny only because of her perspective.

The blanket of stars disguised the vast distance between one star and another. She knew that light emitted from the nearest star system took more than four years to reach the earth. Light from the Orion Nebula had shot through space for 1,500 years before striking her optic nerve. Her eyes were absorbing light generated at the beginning of the Middle Ages.

About 175 years after the glow she was seeing now left the Orion Nebula, a Dane, Ole Roemer, calculated the speed of light. His work earned him a place in history, although only a relatively few people would recognize his name. Her discovery of a new bird species might not make her a household name, either, but it would be recorded somewhere in the history of science and would, therefore, give her a kind of immortality. It was wrong to allow someone else to steal that distinction.

Her resolve strong again, she poured the water into the two bottles, walked to her tent and crawled inside, every muscle and joint in her body aching from strain and fatigue. She removed her jacket and boots and, shivering from the chilly night air, folded herself into the sleeping bag. Despite her pain, she fell asleep almost instantly.

TWELVE

She couldn't move. She knew she was alive and awake, but she felt like rigor mortis had set in. The stiffness affected every limb. Each attempt at movement brought excruciating pain. She tried raising her left arm at the shoulder but couldn't do it. It was like trying to hoist lead. She attempted to lift her left hand at the wrist and succeeded, so she knew she wasn't paralyzed. Next, she raised her right hand then wiggled her toes. So far, so good. Before long, she was able to lift both hands and wiggle her fingers and toes, all at the same time.

Coordinated movement felt like a huge victory. Encouraged, she bent both arms at the elbow. Success. She pulled her feet up toward her butt by bending her knees. That worked, too, although it hurt like hell. She lowered her knees and tried to roll to her right where she could get at the sleeping bag's zipper. The effort took several tries, but she finally did it. After unzipping the sleeping bag, she rolled out onto the tent floor, coming to rest on her stomach.

She lay there for what must have been five minutes before she found the strength to push herself to her knees and crawl on all fours through the tent flaps and into bright sunlight. She looked around for something to hold on to so she could pull herself to her feet. The nearest tree stood about 20 feet away. There was nothing else. She would have to get up on her own.

Still on all fours, she tried to pull her right leg under her so she could use it to push herself to a standing position. Pain shot through her hip and thigh as she raised her knee, but she kept at it until her right foot rested almost flat on the ground, a little like a runner settling into the blocks.

Pushing up with her right leg, she tried to pull her left leg under her, almost toppling over in the attempt. Her left knee struck the ground painfully as she tried to regain her balance. After taking a few deep breaths, she tried again and managed to get to her feet.

It felt awful, like the joints in her arms and legs had frozen and she'd have to walk like the silliest version of Frankenstein's monster for the rest of her life. Shuffling to her makeshift fireplace, she sensed the stiffness in her knees loosening with the movement. Her elbows, too, began to ease as she swung her arms. By the time she reached the pile of wood by the fireplace, she could bend over enough to pick up a few sticks, if she took her time. She found a taller stand of dried grass and tore off some stems to use as starter. Soon, she had a fire going, its warmth helping melt away more of the stiffness and pain.

After lowering her backpack from the tree limb and returning the rope to her pack, she found a package of freeze-dried scrambled eggs with bacon. She filled her two cooking pots at the creek, hanging them over the fire to boil.

The sun had risen far enough above the mountains to shed its full light on her campsite by the time she'd finished breakfast and cleaned her cooking pot. She packed them, along with the sleeping bag, sleeping pad and tent and hefted the backpack up on her shoulders. It hurt, but not as badly as she'd expected. After buckling the waist strap, she started walking north. At first, the pack weighed on her more than it had the day before, but after a half-hour or so, it seemed to lighten.

She knew she was making slow progress and probably wouldn't cover much more ground than she had yesterday, but she plodded on. Rest periods came frequently and grew longer as morning turned to afternoon.

During one of her breaks, she realized she'd climbed away from the creek so she could see over the cottonwoods and out to the valley, all the way to the San Juan mountains on its far side. She shed her pack and jacket and sat on a boulder, feeling the warmth of the sun and the chill of the breeze through her sweat-soaked shirt.

From the corner of her eye, she saw something move. She turned her head and watched a Townsend's solitaire land in a juniper about 50 feet away. It was the perfect chance to try her hand at bird photography with her new camera.

The solitaire nestled into the branches, remaining fully visible and apparently in no hurry to fly away. She removed the camera from the pack, being careful not to make any sudden moves. Turning it on and raising it to her eye, she tried aiming for the bird but saw only black. She had forgotten to remove the lens cap.

Trying again with the cap off, she found the solitaire, but it was tiny in the viewfinder. Fumbling a bit, she located the zoom button and touched it. The bird grew until she could see its dark eye and white eye ring as though she were just a few feet away. She pushed another button, and the camera clicked several times in rapid succession. She'd forgotten that it was set to shoot pictures as long as she continued to hold the button down.

Lowering the camera, she tried to remember how to review the shots she'd taken. She couldn't. Instead of randomly pushing buttons, she found the instructions and figured out how to do it. She clicked through the photos, laughing as each one came up. They were all in focus, sharp and, to her, beautiful. The solitaire's wing stripe stood out, adding bold yellowish color to its otherwise rather drab, gray body.

She clicked through the photos again, then turned the camera off and returned it to her pack. Feeling renewed and confident, she lifted the pack to her shoulders and started walking, determined to rest a little less often and for shorter periods. She wanted to reach her destination and begin her search for at least one living specimen of the new bird.

By midafternoon, after only three stops to rest, she'd reached the point where the creek took a sudden turn to the northeast, up a canyon and about a mile from the trailhead. She had walked about two miles in almost two days, but she'd hiked the second mile in considerably less time. It was progress.

The canyon served as a National Forest campground, but she wasn't too concerned about being noticed. The campers wouldn't be arriving in any numbers until mid to late May. She decided to make use of the admittedly primitive facilities, including the outhouses and a campsite, for one night before pushing on up the mountain. It would be nice to use a seat instead of digging a hole with her tiny camp shovel and squatting to relieve herself. Squatting wasn't something she did well anymore. The day before, she'd almost lost her balance and tumbled into the hole she'd just used.

She found a semi-hidden campsite near the creek and one of the outhouses. The campsite had a fireplace with an iron grill that would make cooking easier. She knew the forest service patrolled the campground occasionally, but seldom on a Sunday. The rangers had better things to do than drive through a place that would probably see no visitors again until Friday, especially at this time of year.

After pitching her tent in the least conspicuous spot she could find, she gathered wood and started a fire. She was almost out of water, so she filled her bottles at the creek. When the fire had burned down to a nice bed of coals, she'd put the two pots on to boil, let them cool and use some of the water to fix dinner — maybe beef stroganoff, maybe chicken a la king, maybe something else. She hadn't had her buttered toast with strawberry jam and her instant coffee since she'd left her house. Her standard breakfast was the thing she missed the most.

She looked up at the right moment to see a Clark's nutcracker fly overhead, it's dark wings and tail with distinctive white patches making it easy to identify. Other birds had come out as well. She could see them — mountain chickadees, white-breasted nuthatches, and more she couldn't identify without her binoculars, which were still in her backpack — exploring for food in the trees and brush. A breeze stirred the pines, and she knew it whispered among the needles, even though she couldn't hear it because of the torrent tumbling down the mountain a few feet away.

Here, the narrowleaf cottonwoods and quaking aspen grew together. Within a half-mile of where she now stood, the cottonwoods would give way because of altitude, and the aspen would take over. Aspen, with their black-and-white trunks were among her favorites, forming large swaths of lighter green among the pines in summer and turning bright gold in the autumn. It would be at least another couple of weeks before the aspens and cottonwoods leafed out, though. Right now, their naked branches contrasted sharply with the pines, laden as they were with dark evergreen needles.

She fed more wood to the fire, pulled her binoculars from her pack, and sat at the picnic table the forest service had provided. Over the years, she'd found that birding didn't have to entail long hikes. Being still sometimes worked better. Driven by curiosity or simply because they grew used to human company, the birds often came close enough for easy viewing and identification. She sat quietly until the shadows stretched long, letting the birds approach. Nothing new showed itself, so she put the binoculars in their case and stood. The birds that had come to the edge of the campsite flew, and she was alone with the breeze and the trees and the rushing water. They gave her all the company she needed for the time being as she started pre-paring her dinner.

By the time she'd finished eating, darkness had arrived. She washed the pot, drew more water from the creek and boiled it. For a while, she sat at the picnic table, watching as the fire burned down to ashes. She was in no rush to enter the tent and try to sleep. In fact, she dreaded it. The agony that had greeted her that morning would probably come again tomorrow. She considered staying up all night just to avoid it, but she was exhausted. She had to rest, no matter the consequences.

Ed stood in the firelight that remained. He seemed to be studying the fading flames. Then he raised his head and looked at her with a slight smile curling his lips.

"It was all a mistake," he said. His words and his gentle smile seemed incongruous. No hint of accusation or reprimand or regret showed on his face or sounded in his voice, only a sort of sorrowful understanding, as if he were there not to judge but to bring her peace.

Instead of disappearing, he remained standing by the fire, smiling. His complacency made her want to smack him. She stood. He held his ground.

"What mistake?"

He said nothing, only stared at her with that maddening smile.

"What was all a mistake?"

His smile widened. "Remember the last time we walked the trail?"

"What does that have to do with a mistake?"

"Do you remember?"

"Of course, I do. You were worried about bears, and you took that stupid gun with you. 'Just in case,' you said. But you'd never been afraid of bears before. I also remember the time you almost shot your foot off when you thought we had a burglar in the house."

The dig didn't faze him. "I carved our initials in that aspen, something I wouldn't normally do because I hated it when other people carved their initials in trees."

"Then why did you do it?"

"I was sick. You knew it, but you didn't want to admit it. I wasn't afraid of bears. I was terrified of losing my mind."

"I know," she said, tears stinging her eyes, her lower lip quivering. "I know you were."

"Why didn't you stop me?"

"I was afraid to. I wasn't sure what you'd do if I tried to make you stop."

"I was trying to fix it."

"Fix what?"

"Everything. What happened, what didn't happen, all the mistakes."

"By carving our initials in a tree trunk?"

Even through the confession, he'd gone on smiling the same smile. It was still there. "It seemed right at the time."

Through her tears, she laughed. What he said sounded like a punchline. But then his smile fell away, and his look turned solemn.

"I loved my work."

"I know."

"And for a little while, you loved what you were doing."

The admission surprised her. She wiped away her tears and took a step toward him.

"You mean the wetland?"

"Yes."

She took another step toward him. "I was so happy then, until . . ."

"Until?"

She dropped her eyes and looked at the ground. "I didn't tell you about him."

"Him?" There was no hint of shock or suspicion.

"Robert Beekman. Professor Robert Beekman. My teacher."

"Good name for an ornithologist."

She looked up to find Ed smiling again. "I think it wasn't. He must have been teased a lot about it, and he got mean."

"So he was mean to you?"

"Not at first. He seemed nice, even though he treated me like something of an oddity, back in college at my age. But one day, he just kind of dismissed me, called me a dilettante."

"Because you weren't going to make a career studying birds?"

"I was fifty-five years old. He was maybe thirty."

"Sounds like he was jealous."

She stiffened at that. Something was wrong here. Ed seemed to be saying the things she'd only thought before and dismissed as ridiculous.

Why would Robert Beekman be jealous of her? He'd published scientific papers, been promoted to full professor before most of his colleagues had reached the assistant professor level. He had been about to astound the ornithological community with a new discovery. But, for some reason, the great discovery never saw the light of day.

"Oh, my God," she said, feeling dizzy but managing to keep her feet. "He was jealous."

Ed gave her a quizzical look. "But what would he have to be jealous about? You were an undergrad. You'd accomplished nothing, really, at least nothing that would earn you a place in the history of ornithology."

"You're right. It must have been something else." She knew it wasn't something else, though. It was jealousy. But what was the reason? Ed was right. As far as her academic record went, it was quite good, but she'd done nothing out of the ordinary, nothing to bring her any kind of acclaim. Robert Beekman had earned the acclaim he'd received. He'd worked hard for it, laboring in the field and over specimens in the laboratory, doing studies, publishing the results, building a reputation for solid research and brilliant interpretation. He should have been a happy man, but she'd never seen him smile beyond a smirk.

She started to ask Ed why a man with so much going for him never smiled, but he was gone. She sat down at the picnic table, frustrated that she hadn't found the reason behind Beekman's jealousy. A female great horned owl called from its perch in the woods across the creek, the roar of the water unable to overwhelm the sonorous *hoo-HOO hoo hoo*. As the owl's call faded away, she felt a deep weariness creep into her muscles. It was time for sleep. She crawled into the tent, took off her boots and jacket and zipped herself into the sleeping bag.

Unable to fall asleep right away, she thought about the conversation she'd just had with Ed. It had seemed so real, and she realized now that she'd been looking forward to it. She'd been hoping to see him again, even though his appearance meant something was wrong with her. During his visits, that didn't matter. She knew he had something to tell her, something to help her understand, even if, in the end, she was only talking to herself.

Later, she awoke to a scratching and scampering sound that traveled up one side of her tent and down the other. Something was using the nylon shelter as a playground. In fact, two somethings were chasing each other, probably deer mice. Chipmunks and squirrels reserved their activity for daytime. Deer mice were active at night. Whatever the creatures were, they seemed to be having a high old time. She fell asleep again, listening to them, somehow feeling less alone.

The next time she opened her eyes, morning light illuminated the inside of the tent, and the deer mice were gone. She lay still for a while, almost afraid to attempt lifting her arms or legs. When she did try to raise her left arm, it hurt, but she succeeded, and she used it to reach across her body and unzip the bag enough to free her right arm and use it to unzip the bag farther. She rolled over slowly onto her stomach and pushed herself to a kneeling position. The effort forced a groan that would have brought other campers running to see what was wrong, if there had been any other campers.

After resting and letting the pain subside, she pulled her jacket on and crawled out of the tent and over the few feet of ground to the picnic table, using the bench seat to pull herself up. Not quite ready to stand, she sat on the bench, moving her arms and legs to stretch the muscles and loosen the joints. Finally, she stood and hobbled to the fireplace.

Pinecones littered the ground. To spare her sore back and avoid losing her balance and falling, she used a long stick to gather them together in a pile. Then she plucked cones from the heap she'd created, using two long sticks as pincers, rather like chop sticks, and dropped them in the fireplace. The cones were quite dry, so it took only two matches to start a fire, which she fed with larger and larger pieces of wood. Following another breakfast of scrambled eggs and bacon, during which she desperately missed her toast and coffee, she cleaned the dishes, took down the tent and packed her gear.

She had brought a toothbrush, toothpaste and a bar of soap but hadn't used them so far. Soon, though, she'd reach a source of water that didn't require purifying, a well tapped by the forest service for campers and hikers. It was at the trailhead, a mile from where she'd camped, too far to walk the night before when her legs behaved like well-cooked spaghetti. Today, she'd have plenty of water for drinking, brushing her teeth, and even a sponge bath before soldiering on to her destination.

Donning her backpack, she left the campsite, following a narrow road up the canyon. The air still held the night's chill, but when she turned and looked toward the west, she saw that sunlight covered about two thirds of the valley. The sun would rise above the Sangre de Cristos soon, and she would probably have to take off the pack and remove her jacket to keep from getting too warm.

Yesterday and the day before, she could tell she was gaining elevation as she walked. Today, the climb seemed to grow steeper with each step. It had been a long time since she'd walked this way. She and her youngest son — for some reason, his name escaped her at the moment — had decided to spend one day of one of his rare visits getting as far as they could on the trail to Darkling Lake. That was five years after Ed died, and she hadn't been back since.

Darkling was her name for Piñon Lake. She wasn't sure why the name came to her, except no piñons grew around the lake. Maybe it was the sha-dow of a passing cloud she'd watched on one of the hikes she took years ago with Ed and the boys as it turned the water from bright blue to almost black. She only knew it seemed right. She'd never told anyone about it. It was her secret, something she could hold inside, something that gave her a kind of ownership but over which she had no control, almost something sacred.

THIRTEEN

S he'd told Tony — there, she remembered his name — about Ed carving their initials in the aspen. He'd laughed and said he wanted to see the place where Dad had done something he'd cursed other people for doing.

It was early August, and the mosquitoes had gone weeks ago. They'd parked near the trailhead and started up the path early in the morning, armed with canteens full of water and their binoculars. Tony stopped walking and raised his binoculars, focusing on movement at the base of some bushes not far from the creek.

"Spotted towhee," he said.

She aimed her binoculars at the rustling motion and got a good look at the bird. Its rufous sides, black head and white-spotted dark-gray back marked it as a male, and a handsome one at that. She'd seen many of them in the woods around her house, all year round, but she always felt a thrill when one showed itself.

"Beautiful," she said, lowering the binoculars and smiling at her son. Tony smiled, not so much in agreement as amusement at her enthusiasm. She knew he thought she tended to go a little overboard in her appreciation, but she believed it was part of the reason he'd become an avid birder. At 35, he just wasn't old enough to appreciate the gift she'd given him.

They continued up the trail, which rose rapidly above the canyon floor and were soon out of sight of the car. The trail allowed only single-file traffic at this point. It would widen later as they traversed aspen groves crisscrossed by spring-born rivulets bubbling up from the earth. The small streams created patches of mud as they crossed the trail, and Tony helped her across them, even though she could have managed quite well on her own.

Piñon Creek wound down the mountain, crossing the trail several times. These crossings needed bridges, but no one had made the effort to build them. Hikers were left to negotiate fallen trees or hop from rock to rock to get from one side to the other. As she remembered it, the place where Ed carved their initials lay just beyond the second crossing. It had been a long time since that day, so she couldn't be absolutely sure.

When they reached the creek, an American dipper took flight, low to the water, and landed on an upstream rock, where it bobbed a couple of times before flying again, out of sight.

"Haven't seen one of those in a while," Tony said. He was living in Kansas at the time, so seeing a dipper would be a real event. The flatlands weren't known for their rushing streams.

"They're pretty amazing," she said. "They have to be a lot stronger than they look to fight that current."

She'd loved to watch dippers since the first time she'd seen one. It was perched, bobbing, on a rock in the middle of Piñon Creek the day Ed showed her the fishing cabin he'd just bought — without consulting her, of course. Neither of them had seen one before, and they had to look it up in the Peterson field guide.

It took a while to figure out what kind of bird they were looking at. It didn't seem to fit into any category. With its short tail, it looked like a fat wren, but it was bigger than any wren they'd ever seen. They could only leaf through the book and hope to spot its picture. So they turned the pages and, after about 10 minutes, found it.

Much of the American dipper's appeal to her was its aloneness and self-sufficiency, as well as its former name, water ouzel. Solitary by nature, the American dipper is one of only five species in the genus *Cinclus* and the only one living on the North American continent, but it ranges from Alaska to Panama in western mountains. The way it gathers its food by diving into the rushing water and picking up insect larvae and other morsels as it walks along the bottom adds to its uniqueness. It's a weird little animal, and she loved it for its strangeness.

The other dipper genus members have taken their place around the world. The Eurasian, also known as white-throated, dipper can be found from Europe and northern Africa to Manchuria. South American mountains are the home of the white-capped dipper and the rufous-throated dipper. In Asia, the brown dipper occurs in the Himalayas, North and South Korea, Japan, and China.

She and Tony made it across the creek on the trunk of a broken pine. Someone had taken the time to cut off branches that might create obstacles, so it was fairly easy. Still, they both put a leg on either side of the tree and scooted along, neither confident enough of their balance to walk upright.

The trail steepened considerably on the other side of the creek, so they were breathless when they reached a more level path through a stand of ponderosa pines and into another aspen grove. As they walked, the rumble of the creek grew louder until it came into sight and they faced another crossing.

"I think this is the place," she said, pointing across the stream.

Tony looked worried. "Are you going to be okay getting to the other side?"

At first, she thought she'd have to remove her boots and socks and wade through the rapids, but then she spotted a series of rocks close enough together to serve as steppingstones.

"I'll be fine," she said, and she placed her foot on the first of five rocks, all wet and none flat enough to give her secure footing. Before Tony could say anything, she had her right foot on the second rock and her left on the third.

She could feel herself losing her balance as she swung her right foot toward the fourth rock. As soon as it landed, she used it to push off so her left foot could reach the last foothold. Her momentum carried her to the bank, and she raised her arms in triumph.

She turned around to find Tony bouncing from rock to rock, crossing the creek with ease. He landed beside her. A grin split his face the way she wanted to split it.

"Showoff," she said.

"Nothing to it."

Tony moved away in search of the initialed tree. She looked around and saw that many of the aspen bore pairs of initials, some surrounded by carved hearts, others with a simple plus sign between them. She and Tony separated and examined trees on both sides of the trail. It took a good 15 minutes before Tony called out, "Found it."

The twinge of disappointment she felt surprised her, and she realized, if she had had a choice, either she'd have found the initials or neither of them would. The tree could have fallen, pushed over by heavy snow one winter. That would have been preferable to this. She stood, staring across the glade at her son who waited, his face showing his triumph.

"Well, come and look," he said.

She picked up her feet as though she had to pull them from the ground like roots and walked to the tree, seeing not Tony but Ed with his knife, cutting the bark, creating a wound that would heal over and leave a dark scar declaring their love for each other.

When she reached the tree, she touched the permanently raised flesh gently, first tracing Ed's initials then her own. She knew the tree sensed nothing when Ed cut into it, but she felt the need to apologize anyway, and she whispered, "I'm sorry."

Tony stood a few feet away and heard her mutter. "What?" he asked.

She turned to him, tears filling her eyes, and Tony stepped closer, placing his hand on her shoulder. She wanted to tell him not to worry about it. She was being ridiculous. The tears weren't for Ed. They were for the tree, forced to endure the blade, with no means of escape. But that would sound foolish and might give him the wrong idea — that she was somehow reprimanding her dead husband and grieving more for a plant than for the man she'd shared most of a lifetime with.

"You okay, Mom?"

She took his hand off her shoulder and held it. He looked so much like his father, the same eyes, the same hair, even the same ears. It was like reliving that day. Except her son wasn't losing his mind. He was healthy, whole, both physically and mentally. She hugged him, laying her head against his chest, holding him tightly for a few seconds. Then she released him.

"Let's go back," she said, and started walking down the mountain, crossing the creek using the five rocks as steppingstones. She hadn't returned since that day.

Now she was going back. She didn't know that the initialed aspen would be there still and almost hoped it would be gone, returning to the earth as all dead things should. The hike would be hard; there were few more or less level sections of the trail to allow progress without labor that would leave her breathless and needing a rest every 20 feet or so.

It would take her at least an hour to get to the trailhead, where she would spend a half hour or so washing herself and changing some of her clothes. The rest of the day would be consumed with climbing to the aspen grove. If she made it that far. She might not have the strength.

As was her habit, she continually scanned the trees, undergrowth, and other cover, as well as the slice of visible sky for birds, spotting a canyon wren among the boulders and a turkey vulture circling overhead.

She was too high for narrow leafed cottonwoods, and aspen had taken their place. Up ahead, higher on the mountain, she could see a large aspen grove that had overtaken a burn area, hiding it like a bandage. She'd read that aspen groves shared one root system, so all the trees in it were intimately connected. The grove was one organism, with the individual trees only appearing to be independent above ground. An aspen grove, known as a clone because the trees are genetically identical, could live for thousands of years. She liked knowing that something could survive so long.

When she reached the trailhead, the sun had had a chance to warm the canyon, and she took off her jacket. The hand pump that brought water up from the well was functioning, so she was able to bathe herself, using a washcloth and bar soap. She changed her underwear and put her other clothes back on, standing out in the open with no worries about anyone seeing her. The cold water, followed by warm, drying sun renewed her energy, so she was ready to tackle the steep trail and took off at what was, for her, a brisk pace.

Before long, she started panting, and she could feel the strain in her thighs and calves. Her pace slowed, and she took frequent breaks to catch her breath, but she felt stronger than she had two days ago. The chances of reaching her destination that day seemed less remote.

An hour later, she felt less certain about her progress. The trail seemed to grow rougher, more treacherous as time went on. She started tripping over roots and rocks and nearly fell twice. Her pace slowed further. It seemed to take an eternity to climb some of the steeper slopes because she had to stop to rest so often.

After conquering a particularly sharp ascent, she sat on a flat rock and took her pack off. Removing the weight from her shoulders felt like throwing off a heavy yoke, and she almost got up to dance with the lightness. But she didn't. She was satisfied with rubbing her neck and the back of her thighs. Closing her eyes, she turned her face to the sun. When she opened them again, Ed sat beside her. She should have been startled, but she only asked, "Why are you here?"

"Why not?" Ed seemed to look through her at something far away.

"I thought you were just hanging around to talk in riddles and annoy me. Aren't you going to tell me it was all a mistake?"

"It was, you know."

She stood up, the movement bringing pain that made her wince. "What was?"

"You know."

"Damn you, you fucking asshole. You never could give me a straight answer. You ran off to join the Navy without telling me what you were doing. That was cruel."

He shrugged. "That has nothing to do with it."

"Yes, it does. It's only one example out of a whole lifetime of examples. You never told me anything."

"I told you I loved you."

She started to cry, and it infuriated her. "Don't try that on me. You said all kinds of things, but you didn't mean them. You just said them to keep me quiet and fool me into thinking I was happy."

Ed, or whatever it was that looked like Ed, sat silent, unmoving, staring through her. She wiped away her tears. "I want to know about the mistake. What was it?"

Ed shrugged. "All of it."

She wanted to hit him, smash his face, cause him so much pain he couldn't stand it, but she sat as still as he did, wanting to know, afraid to know. What would she do when she did know? Would she want to kill herself, overwhelmed by a sense of failure, finally confronting her wasted life? What else could happen when you've been forced to admit that all your years on earth were a mistake?

And who was he, and the rest of that Greek chorus, to tell her that her life had been "all a mistake."? She'd raised five boys, kept a marriage alive — although maybe on life support — for decades, done what was expected of her every day. How could anyone call all that a mistake? She'd lived a good life, if an unappreciated one.

Where were the thank-yous for the care she'd given her family, feeding them, keeping their clothes clean, patching them up when they hurt themselves, tending to them when they were sick, praising them for their accomplishments, setting them straight when they were out of line. None of that seemed to matter. The man she'd given her life to was here to tell her it was all a mistake.

She covered her face with her hands, turned away from Ed and sobbed, giving in to the despair she now realized had been creeping up on her since the first time she'd heard the voice. When she ran out of tears and only the dark dry abyss of her hopelessness remained, she turned back to face Ed, ready to tell him he was right. It all had been a mistake, her marriage, her children, all of it. But he was gone.

Exhausted from exertion and emotion, she stood and lifted her pack to her shoulders. She had this one thing yet to do, and she would complete her task, no matter how pointless it now seemed. She would find another new bird, photograph it, and return with proof that Beekman hadn't killed the last of a new species.

Taking the next step challenged every resource she had. It would have been so much easier just to quit, to lie down where she was and die. It wouldn't be long before someone found her body. In the meantime, at least it would have nourished a few animals and insects.

She laughed at herself. It was more of a cough, and it tasted like ashes. She'd never been one to feel sorry for herself. Maudlin wasn't among her usual moods. No one would call her gay, but at least she'd been able to hide the persistent sadness that had plagued her for as long as she could remember.

Seeing a psychologist or psychiatrist had been out of the question. Someone in the small town where Ed had decided to practice medicine would have found out. His reputation would have suffered when people spread the rumor that his wife had mental problems.

The only person she'd had to talk to about it was her friend Milly. No one else could be trusted. Now that Milly was gone, she didn't have anyone.

Milly tried, but she couldn't understand how anyone with a big house, money, and a man like Ed could be depressed. Sometimes, she seemed insulted by it. When it became clear that the subject might end her friendship with Milly, she dropped it. Their talks after that mostly involved flowers, birds, tennis, their kids, and food. After a while, it seemed natural to keep the conversation light.

She'd had a bad year after Ed had his stroke. She spent much of her time caring for him, lifting him onto and off the toilet and in and out of his wheelchair and bed, cleaning him, helping him eat, and seeing to it that he did his exercises. Her hip replacement became necessary because of osteoporosis and the stress of lifting him many times a day.

During those nine months, she learned to live with chronic exhaustion and pain. Her hip hurt all the time, preventing her from sleeping and causing her to walk with a pronounced limp. By the time Ed had improved enough to use a cane, she needed one, too, but she wouldn't give in. It wasn't a matter of having too little strength in her leg, after all, and she could deal with the pain. It was worth it to help Ed get better so they could make the move to Valley View and start living again. Of course, he died just when it looked as though he might be able to function independently.

If she were forced to admit her feelings when Ed died, she'd have to say she felt relief mixed with her grief and sadness. She felt guilty about it, but there was no use denying it. She wept at his passing but dove into making the arrangements to sell the house and move to Valley View with an energy that was new to her. The large house they'd lived in for nearly three decades echoed with memories good and bad, but she had no desire to surround herself with ghosts. Life was too short, and she was already well past the halfway mark. She had no time to waste.

It surprised her that she could let her old life go so easily. Yes, there were people and things she would miss — Milly, to name only one — but she had to concede that the excitement of beginning again had taken hold. She longed to see the mountains again, to hear the roar of the creek and smell the rich aroma of the forest.

During the time it took to sell the house, she gave away or sold most of the furnishings and had her deteriorated hip replaced. Then she left.

Maybe that was the mistake. Ten years after she moved into the new place, she began to experience periods of loneliness. She'd made a few friends in Valley View, but they were older than she was. Some had died. Others had moved back with their families or into retirement homes. Of her original acquaintances, only Marge and David Scott remained after 25 years, and she rarely saw them, except at the Double Dyke Bakery. Before they'd all grown too stiff and fragile, they'd played tennis fairly regularly. Now they said hello when they met at the post office or the bakery and otherwise ignored each other. Maybe they'd seen too many other people disappear, one way or another, and wanted to avoid going through it again.

As her friends fell away, and she began interacting more often with younger people, like Janet and Matt, she had moments of regret. She had even told one of her sons — she couldn't remember which — that she might have made a mistake, leaving everything behind the way she had. But surely that wasn't the "all" Ed kept talking about. Maybe it was a big error, but it had nothing to do with the 60-odd years she'd lived up until then.

She didn't understand the young people, just as she couldn't fathom the lesbians, but for different reasons. The young people lived as if nothing mattered but the moment. They took nothing seriously.

Janet put out a monthly newspaper with a circulation of perhaps a few hundred. It somehow survived on advertising from a dozen or so regulars, such as the Valley View Market and the hardware store and lumber yard, but she couldn't see it ever prospering. As for Matt, he seemed nice enough but had no direction in his life, no ambition beyond keeping clothes on his back and food on the table. He seemed perfectly happy with his job at the dump.

She knew little about Matt, except the few clues Janet gave her. He'd been in the army, served in the Middle East and moved to Saguache after being discharged and wandering the country for a while. About his service, Janet knew little, except something happened that left him with difficulty sleeping, nightmares and a tendency to overreact to loud noises. No matter how much Janet encouraged him to talk about his service, he wouldn't. As for seeing a psychiatrist or psychologist, that wasn't a consideration. She could relate to that. If people found out, they'd talk, and pretty soon they'd start avoiding him.

She'd heard about all the soldiers who'd come back from wars in the Middle East with something called PTSD. They showed the same symptoms Matt did. They just didn't seem to have the strength of her generation. They let things get to them instead of toughing it out. Matt had let bad times stay with him, rather than putting them behind him the way she'd been taught to do. It was a shame.

But now she needed to move on. She'd wasted enough time. She put her pack on and started walking, her thighs and calves complaining with each step, her breath coming in short gasps as she pushed ahead on the steep trail. She figured she had about two miles to go before she reached the spot where she planned to camp for the next five days. She thought she'd need no more than two days to get back home because the entire trek would be downhill. Now she didn't want to stop before she reached her goal.

Each time she sat to rest, she studied the trees and underbrush, searching for a small bird that might be the one she was looking for. She'd seen a spotted towhee, chickadees, nuthatches and other common species but no sign of the new bird. She'd have plenty of time to look for it during the next few days, though, so she wasn't worried. She knew the chances of finding it were slim, but she felt confident anyway. Where the confidence came from, she had no idea. And she didn't want to think about it.

That was the problem with being by yourself most of the time. You had too much opportunity to think, and thinking led to regret, and regret led to sadness and more regret. She regretted every mistake she'd ever made raising the kids and being a wife to Ed. She regretted not caring more for her mother. She regretted every petty resentment she'd ever felt about her marriage and motherhood. It was a deep well, and it took all her strength not to fall into it. Did that make it all a mistake?

FOURTEEN

By midafternoon she could no longer hear the creek. It was too far away from the trail. She began to doubt she'd make it to her destination, but she struggled on, not sure how far she had to go. The air had turned colder, and clouds obscured the sun and the peaks. She'd begun to see white patches not far above her, the remnants of a winter and spring that could bring more snow well into May. But she kept on, despite the falling temperature and the threatening clouds. She could smell the sharp odor that preceded a storm and tried to press on with as much speed as she could muster.

The rain started falling before sunset from a slate-gray sky. She found her poncho in her backpack and drew it on over her head. The rocks on the trail quickly became as slick as if they'd been oiled, and she had to step carefully to avoid what could have been a catastrophic fall.

A half-hour or so later, the snow came, heavy and wet, clinging to everything: aspen branches, pine needles, rocks and boulders, the feathery heads of tall grasses. She trudged on, each step a calculated risk, practically crawling up the mountain, using her hands to keep her stable and to catch herself should she slip.

She'd neglected to pack gloves, so her hands ached from exposure to snow and a cold wind that drove the flakes into her face, where they clung to her eyelashes. Nearly blinded by the heavy snowfall, she lost her footing several times, falling flat on her stomach, the rocks beneath her bruising her ribs. But she kept moving, knowing that stopping might mean freezing to death.

After what seemed a long time, the snow let up, and she was able to see more than a few feet. To her left, on the uphill side of the trail, a small clearing opened among the aspen. It wasn't ideal. There were no level areas to pitch her tent. So she chose the spot that best approximated level, pulled off her poncho and let her backpack fall to the ground. Trembling from the chill and weariness, she popped and staked the tent, found her sleeping bag and pad and pulled them with her as she crawled inside. After removing her boots, she tugged her backpack in and wrapped herself in the sleeping bag. Having the backpack in the tent with her was risky, but she was in no mood to worry about bears. She lay, the sleeping bag pulled over her head, as darkness closed in.

She awoke to a pattern created by morning sunlight through tree branches on the roof of her tent. The snow had stopped and drops from its melting off the trees slapped the taut nylon and penetrated it. The spray had already dampened her sleeping bag. The rain fly, which would have provided some protection, remained in the backpack.

The storm had cost her time. As hurriedly as her aching body would let her, she left the tent, removed her equipment, and took the tent down. She needed to find a place away from the trees so she could let the tent dry. Snow covered the ground a few inches deep where the pines hadn't caught it but had melted off the trail, and no dripping trees hung over it. She carried the tent to the trail and spread it over a large boulder.

No dinner the night before had left her feeling weak and light-headed, so she decided to fix herself something to eat while she waited for the tent to dry. A brief search led her to a dead tree, and it yielded enough dry kindling and firewood to boil water. After clearing away snow, she built a round fireplace out of stones and started a fire. By the time the tent had dried sufficiently, she'd had her rehydrated bacon and eggs and felt ready to face the last leg of her journey.

The chilly early morning warmed quickly. After eating breakfast, she folded the now nearly dry tent, packed her gear, and set off. The snow had disappeared from the trees and tall grasses and lay in rapidly melting patches wherever it found protection from the sun. It would be completely gone by afternoon.

Two hours later, she heard the creek and knew she wasn't far from the place she would set up her headquarters for the next few days. She stopped, removed her backpack and drank the last of her water. Finding more would be easy. This area offered a number of springs providing clean water. She wouldn't have to boil the stuff anymore.

After an hour, she still hadn't reached the creek crossing that would tell her she'd made it. The stream rumbled to her right, louder now, so she knew she was on the right track. Here, the trail was smoother, wider, and less steep. It passed through yet another quaking aspen grove, naked limbs sprouting from black-and-white trunks, still weeks from giving birth to the heart-shaped leaves whose shaking, rustling motion in a breeze gave them their name.

Overhead, a red-tailed hawk soared, flapped its wings briefly and soared again. Its orange-red tail caught the sun and flared. She watched it flap and soar its way out of sight, headed north. Red-tailed hawks could be found almost everywhere in the country any time of year. Whereas most species got only one page in the *The Sibley Guide to Birds*, this hawk's variations took up two. It was a master of adaptation, and Helen had nothing but admiration for its ability to make itself at home in both city and countryside. It was also beautiful to watch in flight, as were all the raptors.

When she brought her attention down closer to ground level, she came eye to eye with a mountain chickadee, which, next to hungry broad-tailed and rufous hummingbirds, was possibly the friendliest wild bird in the United States. She could put her finger under a hummingbird at one of her feeders, and it would perch there, perfectly happy to accept the support.

As for the chickadee, it started out a few feet above her, then worked its way down, like an acquaintance navigating a cocktail party crowd to say hello. When it reached a point level with her eyes, it stopped and stared at her, moving only when she stretched out her hand toward it. Then it hopped backward on the branch, immediately starting to pick at the bare wood, as if embarrassed at its own standoffishness. She moved on, and the bird followed her for about 50 feet before flying back the way it had come.

Of course, she knew better than to assign human traits to birds or any other non-human creature, but it was hard not to see the chickadee as an empathetic character. It seemed to be reaching out to her, encouraging her to go on and get the job done. A stupid fantasy but still somehow comforting.

The roar of the creek now drowned out all other sounds. It crashed down the slope in front of her, filling the channel it had carved in the mountainside with white water. She needed to get to the other side, but the only bridge was a narrow log that almost failed to clear the rapids. There were no stepping-stones this time. She could see rocks, but they were barely visible in the torrent. If she wanted to cross, she would have to use the log.

Her backpack would make the crossing awkward, disturbing her already questionable balance. She would have to scoot across with her legs dangling. The creek would soak her legs up to her knees, but it would be better than falling into the rushing water, possibly injuring herself on the rocks and drowning.

She removed her pack, took off her shoes and socks and found room for them inside it. With her backpack in place again, she walked barefoot to the log and straddled it. With the weight of the pack, scooting along the rough wood proved difficult. She pulled herself along an inch at a time, using her thigh muscles to lift her body and propel her forward. The pain quickly grew daunting as her arthritic joints reacted to the unfamiliar movement, and the temptation to stop and stay where she sat set in.

Instead, she slowed her pace, which was already glacial, and took extended rests, letting the pain subside before aggravating it again. The water, which she assumed was not solid ice only because it was moving so fast, had numbed her calves and feet. She wondered if she'd be able to walk when she reached the other side.

At the halfway mark, she jammed a large splinter into her right palm and had to take time to pull it out before she could use her hand again. From that point on, she left a trail of blood along the log, marking her progress in red spots and smears.

The sun felt warm on her back and neck, a severe contrast with the creek water rushing around her legs. Once, she tried lifting her right leg out of the water and, leaning back on her elbows, letting it rest on the log. It didn't work. She almost fell off and decided not to attempt the same move again.

When she reached the end of the log bridge, she found herself facing a tangle of roots blocking her route to the bank. The bank itself rose vertically from the streambed about four feet. She'd have to dismount, like a horseback rider, but her legs wouldn't cooperate. They were out of the water but still without feeling below the knee. Her thighs were weak from the work they'd done to lift and move her along. She hadn't thought about how she'd get off the log once she'd crossed the stream. Now she had to figure it out. There were no good options.

To her left, the rocky ground would make for a dangerous fall if she simply rolled off the log. The chances of hurting herself badly seemed substantial. To her right, things weren't much better. A patch of sand without jutting rocks that extended directly under the log would soften her landing, but the distance to the ground on the downhill side was greater. Whatever side she chose, she risked one or two broken legs if she dropped off the log feet first. Her bones couldn't take it.

As she saw it, the only option was to use her pack as a cushion and land on her back. She might still hurt herself, but at least the impact would be spread over a larger area of her body. The trick would be to position herself to land with the pack between her body and the ground.

And there was her camera and her binoculars to consider. She couldn't risk breaking them. Carefully, because her exhaustion left her feeling weak and unsteady, she pulled off her backpack, removed the camera and binoculars and placed them as far ahead of her on the log as she could.

The idea of falling off the log backward terrified her. If she hurt herself badly enough that she couldn't get up or maybe even move, she would die there, slowly freezing to death during the night. She was so close. Dying might have been all right yesterday or the day before, but she had made it this far. So, with some difficulty, she strapped herself into her backpack.

Maneuvering her body until it hurt so badly she cried out, she extended her right leg farther below the log. Her left leg, bent at the knee, rose higher, and she let it drag over the top of the log. Her body angled to the right until she fell, twisting just enough to hit the ground flat on her back.

At first, she couldn't breathe. The tumble from the log had knocked the wind out of her. She knew it, but still felt panicked, afraid she'd been paralyzed. Then she gasped and air filled her lungs. With the air came the pain. From her neck to her ankles, every joint hurt worse than it ever had before.

Afraid she'd broken something in spite of all her efforts to avoid it, she tried moving her arms and legs. The movement increased the agony, but it did reassure her that she hadn't suffered any fractures in her limbs. She wasn't so sure about the rest of her. She might have cracked a rib or even one or more of her vertebrae. The only way to find out was to try standing.

Like a turtle on its back, she couldn't roll over at first, so she tried rocking back and forth, using the pack as a fulcrum, until she rolled far enough to her left to remain on her side. After that, she could shrug the backpack off her shoulders and roll over on her belly. The movement failed to bring on new pain, so she was pretty sure she hadn't broken her ribs or back.

Getting to her knees and standing almost caused her to scream as though she were undergoing some kind of cruel torture. And it was, indeed, torture. When she finally stood upright, she almost passed out but caught hold of the log she'd just crossed and managed to stay upright.

Feeling had started to return to her feet and calves, but her wet pants were slowing the process and making her feel cold all over. She dropped her pants where she stood and stepped out of them, leaving them in a heap on the sand. Slowly, she walked to the backpack, carefully bent down, took hold of it and dragged it to a boulder where she sat and opened it.

She had been wearing the same pants since she'd left her house. It was time to change. Her boots and socks lay near the top of the pack, so she pulled them out and dug to find her clean clothes. When she located her pants, she laid them beside her on the boulder and reached for her socks. The dry fabric felt wonderfully warm as she pulled it over her feet and ankles. Dry pants felt even better. She pushed her feet into the boots and realized she couldn't bend over far enough to tie them. She would have to make it the rest of the way to her campsite in unlaced boots. Retrieving her wet pants and socks, as well as her camera and binoculars, she stuffed them into her pack and lifted it to her shoulders.

Only a short distance separated her from the place she planned to camp, but it felt like miles. Walking even a few feet left her so breathless and hurting she wanted to stop moving completely. After struggling up the creek bank and back onto the trail, she realized she needed to relieve herself. The thought of taking the pack off and squatting was more than unwelcome. It was scary. She didn't know whether she'd be able to maintain the squat long enough or stand back up when she was done.

Beside the trail, she saw a boulder jutting waist-high out of the earth. She walked to it, winced as she took the backpack off, leaned it against the boulder and let her pants drop to her ankles. After expending some effort lowering her underwear below her knees, she held on to the boulder as she slowly lowered herself into a squat. This maneuver allowed her to urinate without soiling her clothes. When she was done, she used both hands to pull and push herself upright, her hips, knees and shoulders screaming in protest. Then she turned around, leaned with her back on the boulder and pulled her underwear and pants back up. The operation required at least five minutes to complete. The pain and stiffness had her moving in slow motion.

When she'd zipped and buttoned her pants, she stood for a while, still leaning against the boulder. She knew she had to move soon or she might not be able to. The stiffness in her muscles and joints was building to paralyzing levels. If she were to creak when she did move, it wouldn't surprise her.

Pushing away from the boulder, she almost lost her balance. Only an agonizing step with her right leg prevented her from going down. For a moment, she stood swaying like an aspen in the wind.

Once she'd steadied herself and felt able to remain upright, she reached for her backpack and slipped her aching arms through the straps. She snapped the waist strap in place and returned to the trail, the one source of pain she could control taken care of. It was surprising how much better she felt with an empty bladder.

Her pace quickened slightly, and she didn't stop again until she found the overgrown path that would take her north of the main trail and out of view of any passing hikers. She wanted to be far enough away that the only clue to her whereabouts would be the scent of smoke from her campfire and the footprints she left in the soft earth. She planned to burn the fire only early in the morning and in the evening when most hikers would not be passing. They'd be just starting their walk at the trailhead or finishing it where they'd begun.

For a half hour, she followed the almost invisible path until she found herself in an aspen glade on level ground at the base of a nearly vertical cliff. It looked almost the same as it had when she and Ed had discovered it more than 30 years before. They hadn't told anyone about it, including their sons, preferring to keep it a secret. It had been one of the happiest days of her life.

Even though they were in their fifties, they'd spread a blanket, stripped off their clothes and made the sweetest, most passionate love she'd ever experienced. Afterward, lying in each other's arms with the warm sunbathing them, they'd talked as they'd never talked before about the kids, about the future they'd share, the possibilities for travel and opportunities to see the birds of other continents, like Europe and Australia. The only thing they didn't discuss was Ed's retirement — the thing that would give them time to do all they wanted to do together.

They'd stayed in the glade for hours, until a sudden thunderstorm forced them to put their clothes on and don their ponchos. She'd left that place full of hope and anticipation. She had returned to it now hoping to find the new bird again and anticipating a confrontation with Robert Beekman over who had discovered the new species. She believed the photos she would take during the next few days would put her in a strong position to make the claim for herself, even though he had the specimen.

The creek was far enough away that she could hear the breeze stirring the pine needles. That sound almost obscured the pleasant noise of water trickling over rock. She had been counting on the spring, and it was still there, just a few yards away, flowing from a crack in the cliff face and forming a pool that became a rivulet and wound away downhill in the direction of the creek.

She took off her backpack and leaned it against an aspen. Removing her water bottles from the pack, she carried them to the spring and filled them then drank from one and refilled it. The water tasted of the rock it had passed through, and she thought it was the best she'd ever had, almost as good as the sex she'd had that day years ago.

The water acted as a tonic, seeming to chase away the pain from her creek crossing and the fall off the log bridge. She was even able to sit down on the ground and pull her feet, one at a time, close enough to tie her boots. Getting up again proved to be something of a challenge, but she managed it and set about building a fireplace. Once she had the stones in place, she set up the tent and arranged the sleeping pad and bag.

From her pack, she pulled the rope she used to hang the pack from a tree and found a suitable limb. Tying a stone to the rope before trying to curl it over the limb worked just as well as it had the last time. Her campsite complete, she removed her camera from the backpack and checked it by taking several shots of her campsite to document her journey.

She decided not to start a fire for another hour or so, just to give any stray hikers the opportunity to pass on their way down the mountain. She'd brought her notebook, so she set about recording notes of her mission so far. She sat on a fallen aspen and, after dating the entry, she wrote:

"Arrived at base camp, 15:30, MDT, after nearly three days on trail. Photographed campsite for verification. Will supply coordinates upon return to Valley View. Plan to search area to north, south and east, devoting one day each to the three directions, to locate individuals of an unidentified bird species that could be new to science. Will begin with area to north tomorrow."

Writing her intentions down gave them substance, and she felt ready to follow through, although exhaustion had settled on her like a lead quilt. She wanted nothing more than to crawl into her sleeping bag and lose consciousness.

But she also knew she needed to eat, so she started a fire and stood over it, warming herself. The sun floated low in the sky, and the air had turned chilly. The heat of the flames made her sleepy but, at the same time, energized her, seeming to ease the stiffness in her joints and reduce her pain. She toasted herself front and back before finding a package of dehydrated beef stew in her backpack and hanging a pot of water over the fire.

She'd set up the fireplace just a few feet from the fallen tree that served as her seat while she made her notes. After preparing her stew, she sat on the tree to eat her meal. It wasn't until she took the first bite that she realized how starved she was. She wanted more to eat, but she didn't think she should use any more of the packaged meals. She'd brought just enough for two a day. To keep her pack as light as possible, she'd decided to forgo any dehydrated desserts. They didn't sound all that tasty anyway.

By the time she finished eating, it was nearly dark. As she had at every meal so far, she heated enough water to wash her pot and the one spoon she'd brought as an all-purpose utensil. From a zippered bag, she withdrew a small bottle of dishwashing detergent and a washcloth. A few drops of detergent were enough to make suds when she stirred the hot water, and she set the pot aside to soak for a few minutes to loosen the last remnants of food. Then she scrubbed the pot and spoon clean and set them aside for breakfast. After replacing the zippered bag containing her detergent and washcloth in her backpack, she hauled it up high above the ground and tied off the rope. It was time for bed.

The stew had taken the edge off her hunger, so she thought she could sleep without dreaming of filet mignon with a loaded baked potato and asparagus spears with a dessert of buttered toast and strawberry jam washed down with instant coffee. But just in case, she loaded her stomach with water, knowing she'd have to get up at least three times during the night to relieve herself. As for bowel movements, she'd find a suitable fallen aspen in the morning and dig a hole so she could sit over it. Even after three days, she hadn't felt the need, probably because she'd eaten so little.

The lack of calories in her meagre diet worried her a little. Already, she felt a bit weak and shaky, and she needed the strength to cover as much ground as possible to find the bird. Of course, she might locate it the first day, in which case she could eat as much as she wanted before walking back home. She held on to that thought as she pulled her boots off and maneuvered her stiff legs and arms into the sleeping bag.

She was right. The urge to urinate roused her three times before sunrise. The periods of sleep between trips out into the night allowed her muscles and joints to stiffen even more, and crawling out of her sleeping bag proved dauntingly painful. Once she'd managed to slip her feet into her unlaced boots and climb out of the tent, she had trouble standing erect. A boulder near the tent gave her the leverage she needed to get her legs under her, but she was left bent over. Her lower back wouldn't let her straighten. So she shuffled, stooped over like a scoliosis sufferer. On the plus side, she found that being bent over already made squatting a little easier.

Although she did sleep, it wasn't restful. She had to lie on her side because of the back pain, and that brought on hip and knee pain, no matter which side she chose. Rolling over in the confines of the sleeping bag was no picnic either. Shifting around sent sharp jolts, like electric shocks, through every part of her body. It seemed as soon as she found a semi-comfortable position and fell asleep, some new ache woke her.

FIFTEEN

It wasn't until first light that she remembered the aspirin. She'd packed a bottle because she'd known how out of shape she was and expected to hurt more than usual. How could she have forgotten?

She struggled out of the sleeping bag, pushed her feet into her boots and left the tent on hands and knees. Outside, she used the boulder to help her stand. Shuffling over to the tree that held her dangling backpack, she loosened the rope and lowered the pack to the ground, slowly going to her knees in front of it.

For a while, she stared at the knot that held the pack's flap in place, unsure what to do about the obstacle. She touched it, noting the two loose ends that fell downward and the bow above them. But she had no idea what to do with them. She tried pulling at one loop of the bow. Nothing happened. Then she pulled at the loose end to her right, and the left-hand bow loop got smaller. She continued pulling on the loose end, and the knot fell apart, allowing her to lift the flap and look inside the pack.

She dug around, growing more and more frustrated but not finding the bottle of pills. Replacing the flap, she unzipped a side pocket and found the aspirin.

The lid to the aspirin bottle proved to be her next challenge. She tried unscrewing it but, although it seemed to loosen, she couldn't lift it off. It just spun in her hand. Ready to scream, she stared at the lid as if a threatening look might scare it into compliance. She'd opened hundreds of aspirin bottles in her life, including this one. Why didn't it open? Then she saw the words, printed in a circle on the lid's top: "Push down and turn."

She did as it said, and the lid came off. She dumped three of the white pills into her hand and popped them into her mouth, swallowing them without water. The familiar bitterness on the back of her tongue made her wince.

Leaning on the aspen she'd used to protect her backpack, she got to her feet. Crackling wood caused her to look toward her campfire. Ed sat on the fallen tree, staring into the flames that hadn't been there a moment before. He raised his eyes to meet hers.

"You're forgetting things. Simple things. Like how to untie a bow knot and your mailbox number. The aspirin. Your sons' names."

For some reason, his words enraged her. When she spoke, her voice was harsh. "No, I'm not forgetting things. I'm just a little absent-minded sometimes. You don't know what you're talking about."

His expression didn't change. Her anger seemed to have no effect. "It's going to get worse, you know. Before long, you'll start to forget more important things."

"More important than my boys' names?"

"Not just their names. Who they are. Who you are."

"No. No. That can't be. The bird . . ."

"It was all a mistake," he said, and he was gone.

She slumped against the aspen and, dropping the bottle of aspirin, covered her eyes with her hands as tears flowed and violent sobs shook her body. Even as the suggestion that she was losing her mind threw her into a chasm of despair, the shaking wracked her muscles and joints. The more she tried to control the quaking, the worse the torture.

She let herself fall to the ground. Maybe the solid earth would give her body enough support to relieve the seizure-like spasms. Having a hard surface under her helped. Gradually, the sobs diminished, and she regained control of her movements. When her body grew still, she raised her head to look around. Everything was as it had been, except no campfire burned.

She lay on her back, the ground hard beneath her. A small stone protruded from the soil and pressed painfully against her lower back. Rolling over onto her belly, she used her arms to raise her upper body and drew her knees under her, one at a time. She crawled the short distance to the aspen and pulled herself to a standing position. This left her hugging the tree with her face pressed against the trunk. It reminded her a little of the times she'd held Ed, feeling his stubble against her cheek.

Tears came again, but the rending sobs didn't. For that she was grateful. But the hollowness wouldn't leave the space around her heart. Even when death had taken her husband, even during her loneliest nights, she hadn't felt this desolate. Now her quest to find the new bird seemed pointless. She should just pack up and go home, maybe check herself into a nursing home or assisted living and drift away.

Maybe it was all a mistake — her whole life. She tried to remember times when she'd been truly happy. One image came to mind immediately: the wetland where she'd spent a full year studying the comings and goings of the birds. She'd been fully engaged then, right up until the day Robert Beekman told her she was a dilettante. That cruel assessment, coming from a man she admired and respected, had crushed her. She had considered continuing her studies as a graduate student, working toward a master's degree and even a Ph.D. But she had allowed Beekman to destroy her half-formed plans with a few words.

Of course, she had quit before. She'd left college after two years to marry Ed and have babies. That was the point of going to college in the first place — find a good man and settle down. She hadn't given it much thought then. It was only when she became fascinated by birds that she considered studying them formally. Ironically, she'd spent about 30 years birding with her husband, the man who had brought a halt to her college education and introduced her to birds, before she acted on her ambition.

But instead of following through, she gave up and returned to the financially secure and physically comfortable life of a doctor's wife. When she looked back on that life, it seemed empty. It wasn't that she didn't love Ed and the boys. She did, very much. But they couldn't fill the void left when she ended her studies.

As she held tight to the aspen, she realized that the year studying the wetland birds had filled a void that had existed all her life. She'd felt it as a small girl, long before she'd married Ed. As a young woman, she'd tried to fill it with her growing family, but the emptiness remained, making itself known in the night and when she had moments alone. Time after time, she tried to ignore it, but it proved stubborn, like a child pulling at her, wanting attention.

Why had she allowed herself to be drawn away from her dreams? She'd always prided herself on being self-sufficient, on making her own decisions. But had she, really? She could have told Ed she didn't want to settle down until she'd figured out what she wanted to do with her life. She could have told Beekman to go to hell or, better, taken the excellent grades he'd had to give her because she'd earned them and gone on to complete her doctorate, maybe at Cornell or another top institution. Instead, she'd made her decisions based on what she believed other people wanted from her or thought about her.

Ed had wanted to get married and have a family right away. Then he'd joined the Navy without telling her and gone away for a year, leaving her, with their son Eddie, to live with her parents. They reunited in Florida, where she gave birth to Harvey, and lived there for his last two years in the military.

She'd hated Florida. The heat oppressed her, especially during her pregnancy, and the roaches in base housing could take down a small dog. Ed, on the other hand, loved it. He earned his wings as a flight surgeon and spent quite a bit of time in the air while she cared for the two children and beat back the bugs. When they left Florida to move back to the Midwest, she could barely contain her joy.

When they arrived in the town where Ed would build his practice, her life soon fell into a routine. He was gone from 6:00 a.m. until 6:00 p.m. most days, doing hospital rounds, seeing patients in his office and, in those days, making house calls. She took care of the three boys and then, many years later, two more. She cooked, cleaned and, when necessary, entertained. Activity of one kind or another filled her days. Only rarely was she aware of the painful void, and the work of taking care of her family served as a fairly effective, if temporary, anesthetic.

Occasionally, she found herself standing or sitting, staring at nothing, the vacuum cleaner running or the clean laundry lying in the basket, waiting to be folded. She'd shake her head to clear it and go back to what she was doing, not knowing how much time had passed and not caring.

As the years went by, the frequency of these retreats grew. While the kids were young, they'd sometimes find her while she was away in whatever other world she occupied. She'd return only when the insistency in their voices forced her to. Eventually, when the boys were gone more than they were home, she found herself drifting off and finding it harder and harder to come back.

Then she read a newspaper story about Eve Waldman, a woman who received her Ph.D. in chemistry when she was 55 years old. Earning her doctorate had been, according to the article, difficult, but not because of the subject matter. Eve's age and gender had more to do with it. She'd had to overcome obstacle after obstacle, including professors who ignored her in class and male classmates who questioned her abilities and even, apparently, her sexuality. She had almost decided to quit a number of times but didn't. Eventually, she completed her dissertation, graduated, and started looking for a job.

Eve was still looking for that job a year later when the interview for the article took place. She felt optimistic, she said, but chemistry seemed to be a man's world. The story ended there, as if "man's world" answered every question.

It seemed important to hold on to Eve's story, so she cut it out of the newspaper and put it away. When she took it out again, the paper had yellowed and tore easily where she'd creased it. Reading it again awakened something that she'd never realized was in her — a desire not only to learn but to acquire real expertise.

Her years with Ed had helped her become a competent bird watcher. She could identify a wide variety of species — male, female and immature. She anticipated each birding excursion with excitement and a sense of joy beyond anything else she did. She had begun to pay more attention to birds' behavior — how they built their nest, what they ate, how they mated and raised their young. The more she knew, the more she wanted to know.

Still, she wouldn't go birding without Ed. It had become a habit for them to venture out together, and she liked having him to herself for a while. The outings, as infrequent as they were, gave them time alone, interrupted only by bird sounds and sightings.

Returning to college and taking the ornithology classes changed all that.

She ventured into the field with her classmates and eventually on her own to study the wetland birds. Until Beekman treated her to a critique of her motivation and purpose, she believed she had a reason for living. She felt free when she was occupied with her study. For a little while she'd had the best time of her life.

Her loathing of Robert Beekman awoke anger, and the anger quickly reshaped itself into renewed determination. She would not give up, not after coming this far. She had put her body through more than she thought she could endure. She had to finish what she'd started, even if it left her empty-handed or even killed her.

She pushed away from the tree as if she were rejecting a crutch and walked as steadily as she could back to the ring of stones that contained the cold ashes of her campfire. After gathering some pine needles and twigs, she started a fire that she fed with larger sticks until she had a healthy blaze going. The crackling of the burning wood cheered her, and the warmth of the flames seemed to sink into her muscles and joints like a balm.

In her pack, she found more freeze-dried scrambled eggs with bacon and set about heating water to make herself breakfast. She desperately wanted coffee and regretted not adding the little bit of extra weight to her pack. A jar of instant would have been well worth it.

After breakfast, she pulled a small day pack from her larger backpack and loaded it with two bottles of water and her notebook. Then she raised the larger backpack, so it hung from the tree limb out of harm's way. She carried no food, preferring to put off eating until she returned toward evening. She hung her binoculars and her camera around her neck and followed the nearly invisible game track back to the main trail, where she set off to the east. She would be climbing higher and hoped to reach timberline in a few hours. She would search a roughly rectangular area on either side of Piñon Creek, covering as much territory as she could in the time she had.

She knew the climb would be tiring. Timberline was at approximately 11,000 feet. She already felt the effects of elevation, even though she still had at least 1,000 feet to go. Breathing would be difficult, making it a challenge to negotiate the increasingly steep trail. She would have to take frequent rests.

As she walked, she studied the terrain. Large boulders jutted from the earth around her, some of them bigger than the Blazer. Ahead, she could see where the trees stopped and the plant cover, now in large part obscured by snow grew low to the ground, protected somewhat from the harsh elements. Only the hardiest of creatures could survive there. She didn't expect to find the new bird that high, but she had to respect the possibility.

She trudged on, speculating about why no one had seen the bird until now. This part of the Sangre de Cristos was a wilderness area, but plenty of people camped here, hiked the trails and fished the lakes and streams. Some of them had to be interested in birdlife. It was as if the new bird had appeared out of nowhere, suddenly making itself visible after hiding for centuries or, possibly, millennia.

She'd read about the finches of the Galapagos Islands evolving within a few years, adapting to new challenges, and African elephants failing to grow tusks under pressure from poachers killing them for their ivory. So maybe these birds had experienced something similar away from human observation. Perhaps the one new bird's visit to her feeder was part of that process. Evolution usually occurs over a long period of time, but documented exceptions were not hard to find.

All that could make for a fascinating study, but it was for someone else to do. Her job consisted of locating a flock if there was one. The chances of a single specimen — the only one of its kind — finding its way to her feeder, seemed unbelievably remote. Even if members of the species preferred a solitary life, they had to mate at some point, and nesting season was near. She wanted to find more of them before Beekman started his search, as he surely would.

But what if the bird Beekman killed was the last of its kind, the remnant of a small population that finally lost the fight for survival, like so many species before it? What might have caused its extinction? Was it habitat loss caused by climate change, taking away something it depended on too much so it couldn't adapt? Being unable to find the right nesting conditions or food sources can decimate bird populations.

The air grew thinner as she walked, causing her to gasp as she climbed a steep incline that never seemed to end. She had to stop three times and let her breathing slow before she reached a point where the trail leveled off somewhat. At one time, not so long ago, she could have made it without a break. But now she'd grown old, and those days were gone forever.

Still, she pressed on, the trail keeping her close to the creek until, above her, she could see bristlecone pines, their tortured limbs bent and twisted. Some of these trees could be as much as 2,500 years old, holding their position against everything the high mountains threw at them. Sometimes, she felt like a bristlecone pine, bent, twisted, stunted but still alive, despite it all.

When she had begun climbing that morning, patches of snow dotted the landscape. Now snow covered the ground completely, so she had to take each step carefully to avoid slipping and falling.

The trek was taking far longer than she'd hoped. So, with some distance yet to climb to reach timberline, she decided to set out on her rectangular exploration sooner than she'd wanted to. She left the trail to stand on the creek bank, searching for a place to cross.

The water foamed and roared. Ice, a thin spidery coating, festooned the rocks. They would be too slippery to give her the purchase she needed. She would have to get her boots wet and could only hope they were as waterproof as the manufacturer claimed they were. A few minutes later, she found a place where sand and gravel had built up enough to create a narrow band of shallow water that reached almost from bank to bank. She stepped into the creek and waded as quickly as she could to the other side, hopping up on the bank and nearly falling over backward into the water before regaining her balance. Not willing to take any more chances, she moved quickly away from the stream.

The course she would follow couldn't send her more than a half mile from the trail on either side. She wasn't worried about getting lost. The creek would always be there to guide her back to her campsite. But at the pace she walked, it would require too much time to cover more territory. She had to take her time. A broken leg or even a sprained ankle could prove fatal.

It had been a dry year, so the snow wasn't as deep as it might have been. She could slog through, although the going proved slow and tiring. The binoculars and camera banged against her chest and abdomen. She couldn't hold them steady because she needed her hands free to grasp rocks and tree limbs to keep her balance.

Besides her muffled footsteps and occasional grunt from exertion, she inhabited a world of near-perfect silence. No breeze stirred the trees, no birds sang. The limbs had been cleared of snow since the last storm, so none rustled falling to earth. A Clark's nutcracker flew over, the white patches on its dark wings and its white tail standing out against an impossibly pure blue sky, but it didn't call, and its wings made no sound she could hear. Despite the pervasive quiet, she stopped often to listen, hoping to hear an unfamiliar call that might signal the presence of one of the new birds.

After about 45 minutes, she decided she must have covered at least a half mile. She had been walking south, so she turned left, ready to take on another half mile to the east before turning left again so she'd cross the trail and follow the rest of the rectangle before heading back to her campsite.

She was climbing again now, and she felt the change in her legs and chest. Her calves and thighs ached from the effort of pushing through about 12 inches of snow while negotiating a steep slope. Her lungs couldn't seem to suck in enough air. The rest stops became more frequent.

After an hour, during which nothing moved or made a sound around her, she turned north, back toward the creek and the trail. Relieved to be walking across rather than up the grade, she soon got her breath back. A few minutes later, she saw movement well below her, in a stand of ponderosa pines. She raised her binoculars and focused on the spot. Another Clark's nutcracker, looking for a meal. She moved on.

The boots she'd bought for this expedition were supposed to be good ones, but they weren't particularly warm. She wore heavy socks, but her feet ached from the cold, and she still had a long way to walk. For a moment she was tempted to hike back to the trail and down to her campsite, forgoing the other half of her search. Then she remembered the renewed determination she'd felt earlier and decided to complete the task, even if it meant frostbite.

Vapor from her breath drifted away in small clouds. The sun, now high above her in the early afternoon, brought a measure of comfort, but the air was cold. She figured the temperature difference between where she stood and her campsite could be at least 10 degrees. A slight breeze stirred her hair and chilled her earlobes where her stocking cap left them exposed. She pulled the hat down to protect them.

The sun had melted some of the snow, and the rocks gleamed with the wet. The water on the rocks reminded her she was thirsty. She sat down on a boulder, removed her day pack and took a long drink from one of the water bottles. It tasted delicious, and she savored it, rolling it around in her mouth before swallowing.

When she'd had enough to drink, she returned the bottles to the day pack and lifted the pack to her shoulders before moving on. She felt better and realized she needed to take a water break more often. It wouldn't do to get dehydrated.

Of course, the problem with staying well hydrated was needing to pee. It wasn't long before the urgency became uncomfortable, so she found two small boulders a little more than waist high with a space between them, put her binoculars and camera on a safe spot, dropped her pants and underwear and rested an arm on each boulder while she squatted. The maneuver allowed her to push herself back to a standing position with relative ease when she finished. She braced herself against one of the boulders so she could pull up her underwear and pants without danger of tipping over. She rested a few minutes, leaning against a boulder, before moving on.

The route she was following back to the trail took her downhill. She could see the creek in glimpses of silvery rapids mostly obscured by leafless but thick stands of reddish willows on the bank.

She reached the creek without seeing any more birds, only the tracks of small animals that wandered from their burrows in search of food. Her boots had kept the water out once. They'd have to do it again.

Her feet were nearly numb from walking through the snow. Tomorrow would be better unless a storm buried the earth at the lower elevations she'd be exploring. All she had to do was get through the next three and a half hours or so. Then she could warm up.

It was two o'clock, according to her watch, so she still had plenty of light left, but she needed to move. Fighting the willow branches, she stumbled along the creek bank until she found another shallow crossing point. This one, too, extended all the way across, so she stepped into the water and waded as quickly as she could.

Once on the other side, she struggled through the willows, catching the straps of her camera and binoculars on branches more than once. The earth had warmed from the sun enough to be soft and boggy. It reminded her of the wetland in late winter, except that the thin air at around 10,500 feet above sea level had her gasping for breath before she'd made it ten feet into the swamp. When she reached more solid ground, she had to sit on a boulder to catch her breath.

It had been a long time since breakfast. Her stomach growled, and she felt a little nauseated and light-headed. But this wasn't the time to worry about food. She'd have plenty to eat back at the campsite. She drank some more water, hoping it would make her feel full. It seemed to help a little, but she wondered if wishful thinking played more of a part than the nutrition-free liquid.

When she stood up, her legs almost buckled, and she sat down painfully hard on the boulder. For once in her life, she wished she had a bit more padding on her hips. Whatever fat there was wasn't enough.

Standing up again, she kept one hand on the boulder until she was sure of her balance before taking a step. She wobbled a bit but remained upright and felt steadier as she started walking. She would have to be extra cautious as she finished the second half of today's search, but she was sure she could make it if she rested often and kept her wits about her.

When she crossed the main trail, she found herself walking out of the shadow cast by the nearly vertical rock face that formed the southern boundary of a valley bisected by the creek. The spring sun's path had shifted to the north but wouldn't reach its summer course for more than a month. Its rays didn't touch the southern part of the valley, so the snow remained deep. The northern side, on the other hand, bathed in sunlight much of the day, and the snow lay in patches, with a good amount of bare ground exposed. Walking proved much easier, and her feet slowly regained feeling. At first, they ached badly, and she wanted to take off her shoes and rub them. But she kept walking and, before long, the pain returned to its normal level.

For more than two hours, she kept to her course, following the rectangular route that would return her to the main trail, then turning west to get back to her campsite. By the time she turned onto the short path to her campsite, it was nearly dark.

Too weary to cook dinner, she didn't start a fire. She crawled into the tent, removed the binoculars and camera, took off her boots and climbed into her sleeping bag. Every bone, muscle, and joint in her body ached, so she took three aspirin tablets and closed her eyes. Her stomach growled, but in seconds she fell asleep.

SIXTEEN

She awoke in her own bed to the aroma of coffee. When she opened her eyes, she saw her table and her big windows. On the table were a steaming mug, a plate with two slices of toast, a jar of strawberry jam and a dish holding a stick of butter. She started to move so her legs could slip over the side of the bed, but something stopped them. It was as if she were trapped by her own sheet and blankets. She tried fighting to free herself but couldn't.

Glancing across the room, she realized the table and windows were gone, replaced by greenish light, colored by its passage through a covering close enough above her to touch. She reached up and felt the roof of her tent and understood why she was having a hard time getting out of bed. She unzipped the sleeping bag and, groaning, rolled out.

It took a full five minutes for her to muster the strength to exit the tent. She tried flexing her arms and legs to relieve the painful stiffness but was only partly successful. She felt like the Tin Man in *The Wizard of Oz*, but a whole can of oil couldn't fully unlock her joints. Eventually, she managed to put on her boots by lying on her back, raising each leg and bending it at the knee. It hurt badly, but it was the only way to get the job done. Then she rolled over, pushed herself up on all fours and exited the tent, her boot laces loose and dragging on the ground.

Standing posed the next challenge, so she found the nearest aspen and used it to pull herself upright. Once the dizziness passed, she hobbled to the tree where her backpack hung and lowered it to the ground. This time, she removed three packages of freeze-dried food — bacon and eggs, beef stroganoff and beef stew. She was starving, and she needed her strength.

Today, she would cover the south and north sides of the trail, starting where she'd returned to the main trail yesterday. She'd try to cover four miles, tracing a rough square a mile on each side. Her campsite would mark the middle of the western side of the square. With only patchy snow, the walking would be easier, so she would make better time.

She only had one pot large enough to cook her breakfast, so she ate the meal in three parts, washing the pot and bringing more water to a boil between courses. The process took more time than she liked, but when it was done, she could feel her energy return. It would be enough to get her through the day.

Like yesterday, there would be no path to follow once she left the main trail. She'd have to forge her own way through the forest, no doubt encountering some rough ground. She'd have to be careful and continue to take plenty of breaks to avoid any accidents that could leave her unable to walk.

After washing her dishes and raising her backpack to dangle from the tree limb, she donned her binoculars and camera and set off with two bottles of spring water in her day pack. The air was chilly, but her jacket and the sun warmed her. After the long night's sleep, she felt as good as she had in years, which wasn't great, but at least it wasn't god-awful.

When she turned onto the main trail, the breathlessness returned as the altitude took its toll. The half-mile she had to climb to reach the point where she would turn south would be the hardest of the day. Every 20 yards or so, she stopped to rest. On steeper sections, she might halt every 10 yards. The sun was high by the time she reached the cut-off point.

After drinking half a bottle of water, she turned south through the pathless woods, stepping carefully around the larger stones jutting from the forest floor while listening intently for bird calls. Often, she stopped to study her surroundings, not wanting to take her eyes off the ground while she was walking, so she could avoid tripping.

Large pinecones littered a forest floor carpeted with the long, brown needles of ponderosas. Ponderosa pines ranked among her favorite trees, growing as much as 160 feet high with dark brown and yellow bark. At this elevation, they wouldn't get that tall, but they were still impressive. Walking among them, she felt a reverence that no cathedral could evoke. She breathed in the trees' scent and thought it the sweetest incense on earth.

One of the ponderosas, a victim of wind or disease, served as a bridge across the creek. It was wide enough to allow her to cross on hands and knees with no need to get her feet wet.

Except for a light breeze that whispered through the pines, nothing stirred. No birds sang. She walked on, finding the going fairly easy. Still, she kept her eyes on the ground, watching for obstacles that might cause a fall.

About 15 minutes after leaving the creek, she stopped, sitting down on a boulder to rest. An American red squirrel chattered and barked from one of the ponderosas, alarmed by her presence. It was the first animal or bird sound she'd heard since she'd left her campsite.

A short break was enough, and she was anxious to move on, so she stood up, waited for a brief dizzy spell to pass, and started walking. It had been a long time since she'd used her legs this much. The arthritis made it difficult to put one foot in front of the other, and the fact that she'd been able to get around the way she had pleased her. Finding another specimen of the new bird might be a fool's errand, but it was motivation enough to drive her. No matter how it all turned out, for the moment she felt proud of herself.

A shadow crossed her path, and she looked up as a raven passed overhead, croaking once. Somehow, the presence of the large black bird comforted her, just as the scolding squirrel had, reassuring her that warm-blooded life did exist in this otherwise silent, almost motionless world.

She recalled that, in some Native American traditions, the raven served as a symbol of good luck and a passage from darkness to light. She didn't put any stock in myths about special animal powers or signs of any kind, but she liked the idea. She wondered how many people, over the centuries, had been able to carry on in difficult circumstances because they believed seeing a raven meant their luck would improve.

Trudging on, taking short steps, her progress was slow but relatively sure. Only rarely did she catch her toe on a protruding stone or need to reach out to steady herself with a hand on a boulder or tree trunk.

When she reached a clearing where a steep, rocky, treeless slope fell away so she could see across the San Luis Valley to the mountains on its western side, she checked her watch. It had been an hour since she'd left the main trail. At the pace she'd been walking, she figured she must have covered a mile. It was time to turn west. She headed downhill, negotiating the slope carefully so she wouldn't lose her footing and take a painful and potentially damaging fall.

In some ways, walking down the mountainside created more of a challenge than the breath-stealing climb. Almost immediately, her knees and ankles started to complain. Her breathing was fine, but the pain in her legs forced her to take frequent breaks. Each step required a search for a secure foothold among the rocks, and she took plenty of time to find the right one.

She could see where the ground leveled off somewhat and the rocks littering the hillside became sparser. As she drew closer to that goal, she grew more confident and came close to pitching forward and tumbling onto the rocks below her. She reached out with both hands to grasp a boulder and managed to stop her fall, but the camera banged against the stone. She wrenched her shoulders, and her arthritis shot bolts of pain through every joint in her body. For a few minutes, she sat moaning, tears flowing, until the worst of the agony had passed. When the pain had eased enough to allow her to move, she checked the camera. It looked okay, so she pulled herself up and made her way down the slope, testing each foothold several times before putting her full weight on it.

She had only a few yards to cover before reaching the bottom of the slope and less rocky ground. She'd negotiated about half the distance when she heard a high trill followed by two quick sharp notes at exactly the same pitch. She didn't recognize the call as belonging to any bird she'd ever heard. Stopping her descent, she planted her feet and raised her binoculars to her eyes. As she searched the leafless brush for movement, the same call came from a different area of the undergrowth. She focused on the spot where she thought the sound had come from. Something moved, just a flicker of wings but definitely a bird. She held her breath and adjusted the focus for the clearest view.

The bird called once more and settled on its perch, giving her a good look. Black lateral crown stripe. Yellow lores. Black lateral throat stripes. Brown eyelines. White breast and belly. It was her bird. The fucking asshole hadn't killed the last one.

She gazed through the binoculars, afraid if she put them down the bird would fly. Then she remembered her camera. She had to get a photograph

Letting the binoculars drop to her chest, she grabbed her camera, removed the lens cap and raised it to her eye. But when she pressed the button that should have enlarged the image in the viewfinder, nothing happened. She had only a tiny image of the bird in the middle of a huge tangle of gray brush. She pressed the button again. Nothing. The camera must have been damaged when she almost fell among the rocks.

Desperate, she tried to shoot a photograph anyway, hoping it could be enlarged to show enough detail for identification. The camera didn't work. She lowered it to her chest and wept with frustration. When she looked up, the bird was gone.

She'd failed. She had no way of proving she'd seen another specimen of the new bird. No one had a reason to believe her. There would be no more chances to make her mark. She was too old, too weak to try again, and she couldn't trust anyone to do it for her. It was time to admit that it truly had all been a mistake, a waste of time. A waste of life.

She stood up. Her legs quivered. Planting her right foot as firmly as she could, she took a step and then another, descending the few yards to the bottom of the slope. When she reached more level ground, she sat on a boulder, weighed down by the burden of her age and a sadness beyond anything she'd ever experienced, including the grief brought on by the death of her husband and her best friend. She wanted to stop where she was, never to move again, to wait for nature to take its course.

A monotonic twitter followed by two sharp notes with the same pitch arose from somewhere in front of her. It sounded close. She had closed her eyes, but now she opened them. The bird, or one like it, sat on a twig not 15 feet from where she sat. She didn't need the binoculars to see its distinctive markings. Anger rose to challenge her sadness. If she'd had a gun, she would have shot the damned thing herself. It seemed to be mocking her, rubbing salt in the wound of her failure. And, although she knew it was ridiculous to think so, it appeared to know what it was doing. Not only did it sing again, but it also turned its back to her and raised its tail, showing all its identifying marks — brown nape, black scapulars, white median coverts, brown primaries, reddish-brown tail and white undertail coverts. Then it shot a stream of white liquid in her direction.

The bird danced on the twig, fluttering its wings, seeming to take immense pleasure in the show of disdain it was putting on for her. At first, her anger grew. Then it dissipated, and she laughed as if she'd just gotten the joke.

The bird was telling her she'd won, after all. Only she knew where this previously unknown species could be found. Only she knew the fucking asshole hadn't killed the last one, that the species still existed in the world.

The bird settled back on its perch then flew into the woods. She watched it until it disappeared among the trunks and branches and sat for a long time staring after it. Once again, stillness and silence settled on the mountain. Her sadness returned, but it was of a different kind, more a melancholy that might come with memories of loved ones now gone. She pushed away from the boulder and walked into the woods, following the bird's route, but she didn't see it again.

After a while, she turned north in search of the main trail. She had done what she came to do — except for getting the proof that she'd done it. The search had ended. The trail would make walking easier.

It took her a half hour to find the trail and another half hour to get to her campsite. By the time she spotted her tent, she was shivering as though she had a fever. She crawled into the tent and wrapped her sleeping bag around her. The shivering soon subsided, so she removed her boots, spread the sleeping bag on the pad, got in and zipped it up.

She'd had no food and little water since that morning, but exhaustion damped her appetite. She slept and dreamed of small birds with yellow lores and a song that was less a song than a demand to be heard.

SEVENTEEN

S he awoke to a man's voice. "Helen, can you hear me?" At first, she thought it was Ed, and she tried to answer, "Of course, I can hear you," but the words wouldn't come. She opened her eyes and saw only the blurry outline of two faces, both hovering over her, too close. Frightened, she tried to pull away, but something held her.

A woman's voice said, "It's okay, Helen, just drink a little water."

The woman lifted Helen's head and pressed something to her lips. Fluid passed into her mouth, and she felt it flowing, cool and delicious, over her tongue. She swallowed and drank more until the woman took it away.

"More," she said. "Please, more."

"Give it a minute," the woman said. "There's plenty more where that came from. You're pretty dehydrated. We don't want to rush things." The woman lowered Helen's head gently.

The man said, "When was the last time you ate?"

"This morning." It was hard to get the words out through her dry lips, and it seemed to take all the strength she had even to whisper.

"Do you know what day it is?" the woman asked.

She had to think about that. "More water, please."

The woman gave her another few sips, then asked again, "What day is it?"

"Thursday?"

"Close. It's Friday."

"But I went to sleep on Wednesday."

"Are you sure?"

"Yes, I'm sure."

"So you've been asleep for almost two full days. It's been that long since you had food or water."

"I was tired."

The man said, "Do you know who we are?"

She tried to focus on their faces, but they were still blurry. "I can't see you very well."

"Do you recognize our voices?"

"I think I've heard them before."

"Okay. I'm Matt."

The woman said, "I'm Janet. You know us."

"Do I?"

"Of course, you do."

"All right."

"We'll be back in a minute," the man said, and the two of them left the tent. She could hear them talking softly, but she couldn't make out what they were saying.

When they returned, her vision had begun to clear. She could see their faces, and they seemed familiar. She tried to sit up but didn't have the strength. The one who said her name was Janet helped her.

"We're going to get you back home, Helen," she said. "But we need to get some more water and some food into you first."

At the mention of food, Helen's stomach growled and she felt hunger pangs. She could hear the man chopping wood. "What's he doing?"

"Making a travois."

"A what?"

"It's a kind of sled, I guess you could call it. We're giving you a ride down the mountain. Right now, let's get you fed."

She'd brought a backpack into the tent with her. From it, she fished out sandwiches and a mix of celery and carrots. "It's not much, "but it'll have to do."

She handed Helen a sandwich, ham and cheddar cheese with mustard. Helen would have preferred toast and strawberry jam, but she took the food. When the sandwich was half gone, she had to stop. She handed it back to Janet and said, "Can't."

"That's okay," Janet said. "You haven't been eating much. You're so skinny. Your stomach can't take a lot."

She helped Helen put on her boots and exit the tent. Near the fireplace, Matt worked on the travois, creating a framework of trimmed tree limbs that would support Helen's weight.

"I have to go to the bathroom," Helen said.

Janet nodded. "Okay. Where?"

"I have a place." She pointed to her makeshift toilet. Matt followed her finger.

"Okay," he said, "I'll turn my back."

Janet took Helen's arm and supported her as she walked to the latrine, lowered her pants and underwear and urinated. Matt kept his back turned, working on the travois. Janet led Helen to a boulder, where she could sit.

"Done," Matt said. He entered the tent and emerged carrying Helen's sleeping pad and bag, which he used as padding on the travois.

Janet gathered Helen's cooking pots and utensils along with her backpack. She and Matt took the tent down and stowed everything in the backpack. They gave Helen some more water and took a long drink themselves.

Matt drew a deep breath. "Ready. Time to go."

He and Janet helped Helen lie down on the travois. Then Matt took hold of the two handles extending from the end where Helen's head rested and picked them up so the end where Helen's feet lay would drag on the ground.

"It's not going to be the smoothest ride," he told her, "but it'll get you there."

He started off, dragging the travois, with Janet bringing up the rear, carrying Helen's backpack. Helen closed her eyes and slept. It was a sleep filled with confusing and frightening visions. Ed was there, in his hospital bed, looking terribly diminished. Then he was in his casket, appearing nothing like he'd ever been in life, his lips a straight, too-red line, his skin like shiny wax. And everywhere birds fluttered and screeched, acting terrified and somehow menacing at the same time. Except the new species. When several of them showed up, they sat placidly by, making their distinctive call that somehow rose above the ear-splitting cacophony.

Once in a while, a woman's voice — a familiar voice — would break through. "It's okay, Helen. There's nothing to be afraid of. We'll be down soon." Finally, after what felt like a very long time, she sank away from the scary images and sounds into a black silence.

EIGHTEEN

She sat on a reclining chair in semi-darkness, her slippered feet dangling. A man occupied the only other chair in the room, facing her
and sitting too close. He looked nervous and unhappy. She didn't want to
talk to him, so she let her eyes wander to the creatures that crawled in and
out of the walls. They didn't scare her. Rather, she found them fascinating
and beautiful, glowing bright blue and red and green. She was far more
frightened of the man sitting in front of her.

"Mom?" the man said. "Are you with me?"

She said nothing, still watching the lovely creatures appear and disappear.
This person didn't belong here. He could bring nothing but trouble.

"Mom? Do you know who I am?"

She fixed him with a glare. She didn't know him. Why did he call her
Mom? The creatures moved in and out of the walls more quickly, their
centipede-like legs undulating in waves, intensifying their activity as if they
were afraid of something. Then, in an instant, they disappeared.

The man leaned forward and tried to take her hands in his. She pulled
away.

"I'm sorry," the man said. "So sorry."

She should have been outraged. She should have risen up in righteous
anger and told him to go to hell. Instead, she sighed, the exhalation emptying
her of all resistance. The creatures returned, entering and exiting magically,
calmer now, lovely and strange.

"All right." She raised her eyes to look at the man. Ed sat in front of her
now. He seemed sad, and she wanted so much to comfort him, to take away
whatever pain he felt.

"It'll be all right," she said, "I'll be fine. Don't worry."

She could see his tears, and they broke her heart, but she managed a
smile and reached out to hold his hands. "We should go birding one more
time."

He choked back a sob, and his hands gripped hers more tightly. "Sure,"
he said, and he stood, still holding her hands. "I wish . . ."

She stopped him, pulling her right hand free and holding the forefinger briefly to her lips. "So do I," she said. "I wish for so many things. But I can't have them." She let her free hand fall to her lap.

He bent down to kiss her forehead. "I have to take care of some things, but I'll be back in a little while."

He pulled away, his hand slipping from her grasp. She held his eyes with hers for a few seconds, and then he was gone. Her attention turned again to the creatures. She could focus on them and let everything else go. But, again, they vanished.

She drew a deep breath. This new place smelled like the hospital where Ed died. She didn't like it, and she didn't know how she'd gotten here. From her seat, she looked around for something familiar. She found nothing, not her table or her corner windows looking out on her bird feeders or somewhere to make her toast with butter and strawberry jam and her instant coffee. She saw only a small room with a TV, bed, dresser, a door opening on a small bathroom, and a closed door looking like it belonged to a closet.

There were windows, but beyond them was only a patch of grass surrounded by low-lying brick buildings. A few benches dotted the grass. A lone bird feeder stood in the center of the grassy area. A few brownish birds picked at the grain, then scattered, alarmed by something she couldn't see. She wracked her brain, searching for the species name. Finally, it came to her — house sparrows.

Three men, one in a white coat, stepped into the room and stopped just inside the door. She ignored them, concentrating on the feeder. The man in the white coat spoke.

"She has rapidly progressive dementia. Onset could have begun as little as a few weeks ago. As I understand it, she didn't present full-blown symptoms until she wandered away from home. It's likely that the stress she's been under accelerated her cognitive decline. While she was wandering — and for some time before that — she was eating poorly and, at the same time, undergoing a lot of physical stress. However, the most likely cause is impaired blood flow in her brain."

One of the other men said, "Can anything be done to help her?"

The white-coated man paused for a few seconds and said, "Rapidly progressive dementia can be reversed with early treatment, but she's past that now. We can keep her comfortable and, with the medication she's on, temporarily improve her cognitive function, but life expectancy for this kind of RPD is a few months to a few years."

She could hear their conversation, but the words seemed to vanish from her awareness almost as soon as they were spoken. She couldn't hold on to them. When they ceased speaking, it was as if they'd never said a word.

The man in the white coat left the room, and the other two walked over and stood in front of her. One of the men appeared to be a few years older than the other. They looked vaguely familiar, but she couldn't place them.

"Mom?" She wasn't sure which one had called her Mom. They both looked very serious, as if they were about to tell her something profound. She smiled.

"Who are you?"

"It's Eddie and Paul, Mom. How are you feeling?"

"Lost. I want to go home." And quit calling me 'Mom.'"

"Okay. Would you rather we call you Helen?"

"That's my name."

The two men looked at each other as if they were surprised at what she said. "You think I don't know my own name?"

"Of course not. It's just that you've seemed so confused."

"How long have I been here?"

"About three days. Do you remember riding here in the ambulance?"

"No."

"It was a long trip."

"I don't remember."

She looked past the two men, through the window at the bird feeder. The brown birds had come back. They were pecking at each other, fighting over the grain. One of them dropped to the ground, choosing to go after the easy pickings there.

She could hear the men talking, but she didn't know whether they were speaking to each other or to her. It didn't seem to matter. Watching the birds calmed her. She didn't have to try to explain herself to the birds. She could just watch them.

After a while, the men stopped talking. She reached toward the one nearest her and grabbed his hand, pulling him closer and forcing him to bend toward her. His eyes locked with hers, and he smiled just a little, looking tentative.

"I'm not going home again, am I?" she said, feeling the tears stinging her eyes.

"No," he said, the slight smile gone. "This is your home now."

The two men kissed her on the forehead and left. The door swung closed, quietly, leaving her alone. She shut her eyes, letting her tears fall.

When she opened her eyes, she found Ed sitting in front of her. "I hope they never find the flock," she said.

Ed smiled. "They will. It's just a matter of time."

"You were right."

"About what?"

"It was all a mistake."

"Everything?"

"Everything."

Ed's smile disappeared. "So you mean me, too?"

"Especially you." She wanted to take that back until she realized he didn't seem hurt by what she'd said. His face betrayed no emotion.

His expression remained neutral when he asked, "And the wetland?"

"Another mistake you caused."

"You're blaming me for your decision to stop with a bachelor's degree?"

"I waited too long because of you. I was too old by then."

"You loved what you were doing."

"Beekman was right. I was just a dilettante playing at being a scientist."

"You were very good at playing the part."

"I never would have been able to use what I knew."

"But you did use it. You discovered something entirely new."

"And then gave it away. Another mistake."

"You shouldn't have trusted Beekman."

"Now you tell me. Why didn't you mention it that first night?"

"I didn't know."

"A lot of good you are."

"You're angry."

"Why wouldn't I be? I wasted my life. When I had a chance to do something important, I let it get away."

"But you did do something important. You just didn't get credit for it."

"I want credit for it."

She glared at him. He stared back, still expressionless. "You gave one husband and five children a good home."

"Almost any idiot can get married and have kids. I could have made a little bit of history. Now a fucking asshole will claim it instead."

For a few seconds, Ed was quiet, still staring at her, his face blank. "Do you have any friends?"

"Milly."

"But Milly Brewster has been dead for years."

"Then no. I guess I don't have any friends, unless you count Janet. But she's so young and kind of silly, and I don't think I can trust her."

"She helped you."

"She did."

"And she asked for nothing in return."

"No, she didn't. But what does that have to do with anything?"

"Just a thought. Maybe you should thank her."

And he was gone.

For a long time, or at least it seemed like a long time, she sat looking out the window at the bird feeder. The little brown birds still fought over the grain even though there were plenty of perches for all of them. Some other small birds with dark gray heads mixed with a few of the brown ones on the ground.

She heard the door open, and a young girl in a light blue top, white pants and thick-soled white shoes with a stethoscope around her neck approached her. The nurse or whatever she was stopped in front of her and said, "How are we feeling?"

"We're just fine, but we'd like to make a phone call."

The young woman pointed to a bedside table and said, a little sharply, "It's right over there."

She pushed herself up out of the chair, struggling a little to gain her balance, and walked slowly around the bed to the phone. She picked up the receiver and stood, holding it.

"Are you okay?" the young woman asked.

"I'm okay. But I need the number."

"Who are you trying to call?"

"Janet."

"Janet who?"

She had to think about that. "Lambert. Janet Lambert."

"Does she live here?"

"Where's here?"

"Colorado Springs."

"Colorado Springs? No, she doesn't live here. She — we — live in Valley View."

"You could try one-four-one-one, if she has a land line."

"What?"

"Directory assistance. One-four-one-one. If she has a land line."

"A what?"

"A phone with a cord. Not a cell phone."

"She only has a cell phone."

"Then without the number, you can't call her unless maybe at work. If you know where she works, you could look it up online and get a number that way."

Helen replaced the receiver on the bedside phone. "I don't have a computer."

The girl pulled a cell phone from her pocket. "I can use my phone. What's the name of the company?"

"The *Valley View Mountaineer.*"

The girl punched some buttons on her phone. "Here it is. You're connected." Then she handed the phone to Helen who glanced at the screen and put the phone to her ear.

To the girl she said, "Thank you. Could you leave now? This is a private call."

The nurse or whatever she was looked offended, but she left the room. Janet's voice came on the line.

"*Valley View Mountaineer.*"

Helen closed her eyes tightly, but one tear escaped. "Hello, Janet."

"Helen?" Janet sounded excited and pleased, something Helen hadn't expected. "You're okay. You sound great. When are you coming . . .

Helen cut her off. "Would you come see me?"

Without hesitation, Janet said, "Of course. Would tomorrow afternoon be okay, if my car can make it?"

"Tomorrow's fine. I have to go now." She looked at the phone, trying to figure out how to hang up. Finally, she punched the large red button on the screen with her forefinger. The call ended, and she dropped the phone on the bed.

The next afternoon, Janet arrived as promised, and Helen met her at the door. Before Janet could say anything, Helen blurted, "I wanted to thank you for being such a good friend."

At first, Janet said nothing. She looked surprised. After a few seconds, she smiled. "You're welcome." Then the smile turned to a frown of concern. "Are you all right?"

"Everybody's asking me that. I'm fine. I just remembered I hadn't thanked you and Matt for helping me, especially you."

Janet grinned at her. "Twarn't nothin', ma'am. Woulda done the same fer anybody."

"Well, thanks anyway."

"Sure . . . By the way, I have your camera. It's a really nice one. I took your backpack to my place. Hope you don't mind."

"No, no, that's fine. You didn't bring the camera with you?"

"I didn't think you'd need it, I guess, and I thought it might be too much of a temptation for some of the staff here at the . . ."

"Home? Go ahead. You can say it."

"Helen, I'm sorry."

Helen sighed. "Me, too. Thanks for taking care of my camera, not that I had any pictures or that they would have changed anything. I broke it before . . ." She looked down at the floor and then back at Janet whose eyes showed her surprise and something else, something like joy.

"Wait," she said, "are you saying you could have had pictures? That you found the flock?"

"I broke the camera just before I spotted the birds."

"That's terrible." Janet hesitated before continuing. "But you know there are more of them. That's great."

Then she frowned and reached out to rest her hand on Helen's shoulder. "Not to rub salt in the wound, but Beekman has already published an online paper about the bird you discovered. He even included photos of it on one of your feeders. I was going to call you about it, but I just found out this morning."

"He killed it while he was in my yard. Shot it."

"So that's why we found that same feeder, broken, by the garage. Why didn't you tell me?"

"I didn't want you trying to talk me out of doing what I had to do." She frowned. "Wait. You were at my house?"

"I guess it's lucky Matt decided to fix that broken garage window. He saw your car."

"You were at my house? I told you I'd have the window fixed when I got back."

Janet removed her hand from Helen's shoulder. "Well, it's lucky Matt and I didn't listen. How do you think we figured out where you'd gone? You told me you'd seen the bird fly up toward the campground every time it showed up and thought it might be heading back to join the flock."

Janet hesitated again, then said, "There's something I need to tell you, and I hope you won't be mad."

"I'm already mad at you."

Janet dismissed her words with a wave of her hand. "What you told me about Beekman — it made me not trust him."

Janet paused, and her eyes seemed to plead for understanding. "Go on," Helen said.

"I was taking photos that day when you thought I was having car trouble."

"You took pictures of the bird?"

"My camera was handy, so yes."

Helen stared at her, a realization dawning. She almost smiled but repressed it.

"But Beekman doesn't have the pictures you took."

"No, he doesn't. He probably thought you didn't have any evidence besides your description of the bird. And that means we can prove you saw it before he did. Every photo on my camera is stamped with the date and time it was taken. The chances are very good that Beekman's are, too. You documented the new bird a week before Beekman shot his own photos and then killed the bird."

Helen sighed. "It doesn't matter."

"Of course, it matters. You have to fight this."

Helen paused, looked away and then held Janet's eyes with her own. "Listen, Janet. There's something wrong with me, with my mind. I have trouble remembering things. I get confused."

Janet's eyes widened, and she gasped as if she'd been struck. "But you sound so much better than you did when we found you."

"They're giving me medicine, but it'll stop working pretty soon. I don't have time."

Janet reached out, placing a hand on each of Helen's shoulders. Tears caused her eyes to glimmer. "Oh, my God. Helen, I'm so sorry."

"Don't be. It's just the way things are. I made a mistake."

When Janet replied, her voice sounded angry. "No, Robert Beekman made the mistake, and we're going to make things right."

"Please, Janet, just let it go."

"I can't. I might only be editor of a small-town newspaper, but I'm still a journalist. It's my job to expose people like Beekman. So I'm going to do it. If I have anything to say about it, that bird's story is going to change."

Helen grasped her right hand. "I wish you wouldn't."

Janet, her expression at first angry then softening into sorrow, nodded. "Okay."

"At least, not until I'm dead." Helen smiled at the change in Janet's expression from sad resignation to shocked recognition. "Don't worry. The doctors say it shouldn't be more than a few months to a year. Just enough time for Beekman to bask in his glory and spread his lies for a while."

Janet shook her head and held Helen's gaze. "But don't you want to be around to see the shit hit the fan?"

"I probably wouldn't notice anyway. But I don't want to be bothered." She smiled again, more broadly. "Potty mouth."

Laughing, Janet took Helen in her arms. At first, Helen tried to pull away, but Janet only held her more tightly. Finally, Helen let herself wrap her arms around Janet. She rested her head on Janet's shoulder, her tears wetting Janet's hair and shirt.

"I love you," she said.

Janet pulled her closer. "I love you, too. I don't want you to go, no matter how hard you are to get along with."

Helen laughed and then sobbed, tightening her hold as well. She didn't want the moment to end. The thought of releasing Janet caused almost un-bearable pain, a kind of suffering that exceeded anything she'd known. Janet seemed to absorb it all, becoming like a poultice that could draw it away but not without inflicting its own hurt.

During the hour or so that followed, they sat on the edge of the bed, Janet holding both of Helen's hands and talking about the goings on in Valley View and how much Helen was missed. For her part, Helen remained mostly silent. She didn't believe for a moment that anyone missed her all that much. She had no illusions about how likeable she was. On the other hand, she did miss Valley View, especially her house and her birds — and her buttered toast with strawberry jam and the occasional Double Dyke croissant. When Janet left, they both cried a little and held each other close.

After the door closed behind Janet, Helen turned around and caught sight of her reflection in the mirror over her dresser. She approached her own image, noting her nearly snow-white hair and the deep wrinkles that made her cheeks look like the craggy mountain faces that rose behind her house. To her eyes, she looked as old as those fissured peaks.

She shifted her gaze away from the mirror then, reluctantly, back.

"You did it." Ed stood beside her in the mirror, his eyes holding hers in their reflection, his voice soft.

With a calm that surprised her, Helen replied, "You mean it wasn't all a mistake?"

"Not anymore. It could have been, but you changed it."

"Changed what? I won't ever be able to name my new bird or tell the story about discovering it."

"You mean you won't be famous in your own small way. You won't get the revenge you want."

"No, I won't. At least, I won't experience it. It's up to Janet to tell the story now."

"And she will. Not because she particularly cares about new bird species or scientific integrity."

"Then why?"

"Because she cares about you in a way no one else has."

"Even you?"

Ed said nothing, just held her eyes with his, showing no emotion. For a moment, a profound grief washed over her, and she nearly went to her knees, an action that she knew would cause intense pain. She caught herself and straightened. Wiping away her tears before they could fall, she smiled and said, "I knew that."

She turned toward Ed, but he was gone.

NINETEEN

For a while, the people who came and went seemed familiar, but she had trouble recalling their names. They called her "Mom" or "Helen," and they treated her kindly. She tried to talk to them, but she got lost in their words and just said whatever came to mind. They'd ask her what she meant, but she couldn't tell them because she didn't know herself. Finally, she stopped trying.

From her chair, she could watch the bird feeder through the window. It was close enough that she could see the birds quite well, even without her binoculars, which she couldn't find anyway.

She rarely left the chair, except for a few meals in the dining room, where she sat with strangers. The food was okay, but she found herself longing for toast with butter and strawberry jam. She could almost taste it. But when she asked for it, she was told it wasn't on the menu.

One day, a young woman visited her — another familiar face without a name. Helen thought the woman had come around before, but she couldn't remember when or why. This time the woman brought a paper bag.

"I had the people in the kitchen warm this up for you," she said.

To Helen, the words were a jumble of meaningless sounds. The young woman opened the bag and removed something that smelled delicious. Helen closed her eyes and inhaled the aroma of warm pastry.

When she opened her eyes, the woman had laid the pastry on the flattened bag and placed an open packet of strawberry jam and a plastic knife beside it on the overbed table. "A croissant from Minnie and Tilly."

Helen reached for the croissant and almost knocked it off the table. The woman rescued it before it hit the floor and placed it and the bag back where they came from.

"I'm sorry," Helen said.

"It's okay." The woman seemed pensive now. "Helen, do you know who I am?"

After studying the woman's face, Helen said, "I've seen you before."

A tear formed in the corner of the woman's right eye. She quickly brushed it away.

"I'm Janet."

Helen paused, studying the woman. "Janet."

The woman who called herself Janet sat on the edge of the bed. "I'm sorry I didn't come back sooner," she said.

Helen took her hand. "It's okay. I haven't been myself. Would you like part of my croissant? Someone brought it."

Janet looked terribly sad. "No, no. You enjoy it. I'll just sit here and keep you company."

Helen smiled at her. "That would be nice." She tore off a piece of her pastry, spread some jam on it and put it in her mouth, her expression one of blissful delight.

The woman who called herself Janet stayed while Helen finished her croissant. Then she stood, put the bag, jam container and plastic knife in the trash and took Helen's hand. "It's time for me to go," she said.

Helen felt a pang in her chest, a reaction that surprised her. After all, she barely knew this woman. But she smiled and tried to look sorry to see the woman go as she walked out the door. Then she pushed the overbed table out of the way and turned her attention to the feeder in the yard beyond the window where brown birds fought with each other for a perch.

A new bird joined the flock. It was about the same size as the brown ones, but its plumage was different. It had more white than the others and a reddish tint on its tail. For a little while, it pecked at the grain. Then it flew directly at her. She was afraid it would crash into the window, but it passed through the glass as if it weren't there.

The bird flew around the room as though exploring it, getting closer to her in diminishing circles. Fascinated, she followed its graceful, surprisingly slow flight. It seemed familiar, but she couldn't name its species.

It landed on her right leg, perched above her knee and appeared to study her, its head tipping first left then right, like a dog, in a way that seemed quizzical. She reached out to touch the bird, and it let her stroke the back of its head with her index finger.

"Aren't you a pretty little thing," she said. The bird responded with a trill followed by two quick notes, the tone of the trill and both notes identical.

She stopped stroking the bird's head and glared at it. "So you've come to tease me again, have you?"

The bird stared back at her, and she softened. She resumed stroking it gently and picked it up, cradling it in her hand, and continued stroking it gently.

"You should leave now. Some fucking asshole might shoot you. You need to go back where you came from and stay there."

The bird seemed unperturbed, stretching its neck like a cat luxuriating in the touch of her finger. Then it shook itself, fluttered its wings and flew, unharmed, through the window glass and toward the mountains, disappearing into the setting sun.

She felt its going, not from her hand but from her heart. She knew she would never see it again. In its wake, the new bird carried all her pain away. Her eyelids falling closed, she let her breath escape one last time.

About the Author

During his career, Christopher Ryan has been a children's author, screenwriter, novelist and educator. He holds a master's degree in English from the University of Kansas, where he graduated with highest distinction and was inducted into the honor societies of Phi Beta Kappa and Phi Kappa Phi. He lives with his wife Fran, a psychologist, in Kansas City, Missouri.

Dear Reader,

Two years after I left the U.S. Navy and returned to college, my dad suffered a brain hemorrhage. He died about eight months later. During that time, my mom nearly killed herself caring for him.

Discovery is a product of those months, the years that preceded them and the period after Dad's death. The story as I tell it is fiction, but much of what happens to the characters is true. Fiction is wishful thinking about the good that could be, but it can't get around the bad that has been and will be. *Discovery,* because it tells the story of human beings, can't separate the two.

I hope readers will enjoy getting to know Helen Bryan in all her irascible, stubborn, ambitious, frustrated, frustrating and complicated womanhood. Like many of the characters in *Discovery,* Helen is a real person, but the story is biography written to honor what might have been and to keep the possible alive.

During my career, I have been the author of three children's books about world landmarks. I've written a number of screenplays, including three that have been produced, including *Raising Jeffrey Dahmer,* the story of the serial killer's father; *Hope* (ghostwritten), a film about the struggle of an injured young man to get stem-cell treatment; and *Drifter: Henry Lee Lucas,* the story of the self-proclaimed most prolific serial killer ever known. I've also been an educator and now, a novelist. Discovery is my first published novel. Two more, *Catching Out* and *Cuckoo* are nearing completion.

I live in Kansas City, Missouri, with my wife Fran, a psychologist. We're both avid birders.

Christopher Ryan